COURTING RUTH

Emma Miller

Steeple
Hill®

Published by Steeple Hill Books™

STEEPLE HILL BOOKS

Steeple
Hill®

ISBN-13: 978-0-373-87624-2

COURTING RUTH

www.SteepleHill.com

Printed in U.S.A.

"Are you all right?" the stranger demanded.

Unable to find her voice, Ruth nodded.

He lifted her into his arms, and gazed into her face.

Ruth couldn't catch her breath. All she could do was stare into the most beautiful blue eyes she had ever seen.

"You scared me half to death," he murmured, still holding her.

"Is she hurt?"

The sound of her mother's voice brought her back to the reality of the situation. "Put me down," she ordered, embarrassed now. "I'm fine."

Flustered, Ruth stuffed her loose red hair up in her *Kapp*.

"You sure you're all right?" The beautiful stranger looked boldly into her face.

The man staring at her was entirely too handsome. He was tall and broad shouldered, with a dimple on his chin. He was clean-shaven, so he wasn't married.

"Eli Lapp." He offered his hand to her the way the English did, but she didn't take it.

Another flush of embarrassment crept across her face.

"And you must be Ruth, Hannah's daughter," he said, grinning.

How did he know Mam? How did he know her?

EMMA MILLER

lives quietly in her old farmhouse in rural Delaware amid the fertile fields and lush woodlands. Fortunate enough to be born into a family of strong faith, she grew up on a dairy farm, surrounded by loving parents, siblings, grandparents, aunts, uncles and cousins. Emma was educated in local schools, and once taught in an Amish schoolhouse much like the one at Seven Poplars. When not caring for her large family, reading and writing are her favorite pastimes. *Courting Ruth,* the first in her Hannah's Daughters series, is her first romance for Love Inspired.

May you be blessed by the Lord, my daughter; this last instance of your loyalty is better than the first.

—*Ruth* 3:10

For my great-grandmother Emma, a woman of deep faith, enduring love, and legendary might.

Chapter One

Spring... Kent County, Delaware

Ruth Yoder lifted her skirt and deftly climbed the wooden stile at the back corner of the fence that marked the property line between her family's farm and their nearest neighbor. The sun-warmed boards felt good on the soles of Ruth's bare feet, bringing back sweet memories and making her smile. *Dat's stile, God rest his soul.* How she missed him. The world had always seemed safe when her father was alive. Without him at the head of the table, life was more uncertain.

What *was* certain was that if they didn't hurry, recess would be over, and Mam wouldn't get her lunch. "Come along, Susanna," she called over her shoulder to her sister.

"Come along," Susanna repeated as she scampered up the stile, clutching their mother's black lunch pail tightly in one chubby hand. Susanna would be eighteen in a few months. She should have been able to carry the lunch across the field to the schoolhouse unaccompanied, but in many ways, she would always be a child.

The English said Susanna had Down syndrome or called

her a special-needs person, but Dat had always said that she was one of the Lord's gifts and that they should feel blessed every day that He had entrusted her to their family. Susanna's chubby face and slanting blue eyes might seem odd to strangers, but to Ruth, her dear little face, framed by the halo of frizzy red hair that marked her as one of Jonas Yoder's seven daughters, was beautiful.

Susanna's white *Kapp* tied over her unruly bun, her Plain blue dress and white apron were exactly like those that Mam had sewn for Ruth. But Susanna's rosy cheeks, stubby little feet and hands and bubbly personality made her unlike anyone that Ruth had ever known.

Sometimes, to her shame, Ruth secretly felt the tiniest bit of envy for her sister's uncomplicated world. Ruth had to struggle every day to be the kind of person her mother and her church expected. Being a good soul just seemed to come naturally to Susanna. Ever since her sister Johanna had married and moved to her husband's farm down the lane, the responsibility of being the oldest child had settled heavily on Ruth's shoulders. It was that sense of responsibility that had caused her and Mam to have words after breakfast this morning. Not an argument exactly, but a disagreement, and that conversation with her mother made her stomach as heavy as one of Aunt Martha's pecan-raisin pies.

"You're twenty-three out, Ruth," Mam had reminded her as she'd taken her black bonnet from the hook and tied it over her *Kapp* before starting off for school. "You joined the church when you were nineteen. You've done a woman's job in our house since you were fifteen. It's past time you chose a husband and had your own home."

"But you need me here," she had insisted. "Without Dat, running the farm, taking care of Susanna and teaching school is too much for you. It's better that I remain single and stay with you."

"Fiddle-faddle," Mam had said as she'd gathered her books.

"...Roofie! You're not listening to me."

"*Ya,* I am." Ruth shook off her reverie and steadied her sister as she descended the steps on the far side of the fence.

"But you're not. Look!" Susanna pointed. Above the trees, in the direction of the school, rose a column of smoke.

"Samuel's probably burning brush."

"But, Roofie." Susanna trotted to keep up with Ruth's longer strides as they followed the narrow path through the oak grove. "I smell smoke."

"Mmm-hmm," Ruth answered absently. Tonight she would apologize to her mother and—

"Fire!" Susanna squealed as they entered the clearing surrounding the one-room schoolhouse. "The school is on fire!"

Ruth's mouth gaped in astonishment. Ahead, clouds of smoke billowed from the front porch and cloakroom of the neat, white schoolhouse. In the field, behind an open shed, Ruth spotted the children engaged in a game of softball. Upwind of the building, no one had smelled the smoke yet.

"Sit down, Susanna," Ruth ordered. "Sit here and guard Mam's lunch."

"But the school—" her sister protested, hopping on one bare foot and then the other.

"Don't move until Mam or I come for you."

Susanna sighed heavily but dropped to the ground.

Thank You, Lord, Ruth thought. If there was one thing she could depend on, it was that Susanna would always do as she was asked, so at least she wouldn't have to worry about her safety. Closer to the school than the field, Ruth ran toward the burning structure, bare feet pounding the grass, the skirt of her dress tugging at her knees.

As she drew closer, she saw Mam's new student, Irwin Beachy, crawl out from under the porch. His face and shirt were smudged black, and he was holding his hands out awkwardly, as though they'd been burned.

"Irwin? What happened? Are you hurt?" she called to him.

The boy's eyes widened in terror. Without answering, he dashed away toward the woods.

"Irwin!" Ruth shouted. "Come back!"

When the boy vanished in the trees, she turned back to the school. An ugly crackling noise rose and flames rippled between the floorboards of the front porch. Through the open door, she could see tongues of red flame shimmering through the black smoke. The cloakroom seemed engulfed in fire, but the thick inner door that led to the single classroom was securely closed.

Wrapping her apron around her hands to protect them, Ruth grabbed the smoking rope that dangled from the cast-iron bell by the steps. She yanked hard, and the old bell pealed out the alarm. Then she released the rope and darted to the hand water pump that stood in the yard.

By the shouts and cries coming from the ball field, Ruth knew that the children had heard the bell and seen the smoke. By school age, every Amish child knew what to do in case of a fire, and she was certain they would arrive in seconds. She pumped hard on the handle of the water pump, filling the bucket that always sat there, and then ran back to dash the water onto the front wall of the school. Two of the older boys pounded up behind her. Toby Troyer pulled off his shirt and beat at the flames with it. Vernon

Beachy grabbed the empty bucket from Ruth's hands and raced back to refill it.

Ruth's mother directed the fire-fighting efforts and instructed the older girls to take the smaller children back to where Susanna waited so that they would be out of danger.

Two of the Beachy boys carried the rain barrel to the other side of the schoolhouse and splashed water against the wall. Other boys used their lunch buckets to carry water. One moment they seemed as if they were winning the battle, but the next moment, flames would shoot up in a new spot. Someone passed her a bucket of water, and Ruth rushed in to throw it on the porch roof. As long as the roof didn't catch fire, the building might be saved. Abruptly, a sensation of heat washed up over her. She glanced down to see that sparks had ignited the hem of her apron.

As she reached down frantically to tear off the smoldering apron, strong hands closed around her waist and lifted her off the ground. Before she could utter a protest, Ruth found herself thrown onto the ground and roughly rolled over and over in the grass. Her bonnet came off, her hairpins came loose, and her hair tumbled down her back.

"Are you trying to kill yourself? Didn't you see your apron on fire?" A stranger with the face of an angel lifted her into his arms, and gazed into her face.

Ruth couldn't catch her breath. All she could do, for a second, was stare into the most beautiful blue eyes she had ever seen. Behind her she heard the shouts of male voices, but she couldn't tear her gaze from the eyes.

"Are you all right?"

She swallowed hard, unable to find her voice, and nodded as she began to cough.

"You scared me half to death," he murmured, still holding her against him, his body as hot against hers as the flames of the fire behind them.

"Is she hurt?" Mam laid a hand on Ruth's arm as her rescuer backed away from the smoking building.

The sound of her mother's voice brought her back to the reality of the situation. "Put me down," she ordered, embarrassed now. "I'm fine."

"Her apron was on fire. Her clothes would have gone up next," he explained, lowering Ruth gently until her bare feet touched the ground.

"It looks like the fire's almost out," Mam said, turning to see Roman and one of the older boys spraying the back wall with fire extinguishers. "Thank goodness they were able to climb in the window and get the extinguishers."

Ruth snatched off her ruined apron and accepted her *Kapp* that Mam handed her. Flustered, she stuffed her loose hair up in the dirty *Kapp,* stabbing the pins she had left into the hastily gathered knot of red hair.

"You sure you're all right?" The beautiful stranger was beside her again. He cupped a strong hand under her chin, tilted her head up and looked boldly into her face.

Ruth bristled and brushed away his hand. The man staring at her was no angel and entirely too handsome for his own good. He was tall and broad-shouldered, with butter-yellow hair that tumbled over one eye and a dimple on his square chin. He was clean-shaven, she noticed, so he wasn't married, although he was certainly old enough.

She choked and coughed again, more flustered by his familiarity than by the smoke still lingering in her mouth and lungs.

"Eli Lapp." He offered his hand to her the way the English did, but she didn't take it.

Another flush of embarrassment crept across her face.

"And you must be Ruth, Hannah's daughter," he said, letting his hand drop, but still grinning.

Ruth looked to her mother, feeling a betrayal of sorts. Mam knew this Eli? How did he know Mam? How did he know Ruth?

A hint of unease flashed across her mother's face, quickly replaced with her normal calm. "Eli is Roman's sister's son. He's come from Belleville, Pennsylvania, to work for Roman. We met at the chair shop yesterday. Thank the Lord he was close enough to help. You might have been badly burned."

"I didn't need rescuing," she protested. She didn't want to be beholden to this arrogant stranger who made her feel so foolish. "I saw the sparks. I was taking my apron off when he threw me on the grass."

"Nevertheless, I thank God that he sent someone to watch over you." Mam squeezed her hand. "I don't know what I'd do without you."

Mam turned to face the school. The fire seemed to be out, and the men had set aside the fire extinguishers. "I just don't see how this could have happened. We haven't had a fire in the stove in weeks, and we have no electricity."

"I'd say somebody started it," Eli replied. "That's how this kind of thing usually happens."

Immediately, Ruth thought of Irwin Beachy, who she'd seen running away from the school, but she didn't say anything. Irwin had a reputation for causing trouble. He'd been a thorn in Mam's classroom ever since he'd come from Ohio to live with his cousins after his parents had died. But Irwin could have just been frightened by the fire. It would be wrong to accuse him, especially in front of this Eli.

"It was good you came when you did," Mam said to

Roman as he approached. "God must have sent you. If it wasn't for you, we might have lost the school."

"We were delivering a table to Esther Mose. We heard the bell." Roman glanced at Ruth. "Good you thought to ring it." He slapped Eli's shoulder. "And good my nephew saw Ruth's clothes catch fire."

"Glad to be of service." Eli stared boldly at Ruth and she felt heat wash over her again. "I'd hate to see such a pretty face burned."

Ruth felt so self-conscious that she wanted to melt into the grass. "We're thankful God sent you to save the school," she said stiffly.

"No lives were lost and no one was injured," Mam said. "Wood can be replaced." She straightened her shoulders. "It appears we'll be in need of a good carpenter. We're nearly at the end of the school term, and the children can't miss any days, especially those who are graduating."

Eli winked at Ruth. Even with her face smudged with soot and her red hair all in a tangle, she was the prettiest girl he'd ever laid eyes on. She had the cutest little freckled nose and a berry-colored mouth. She wasn't very tall; her head came barely to the top of his shoulder, but she was slim and neatly put together in her modest blue dress. But most of all, he was drawn to her eyes, nutmeg brown with dashes of cinnamon and ginger. "Aren't you a little old to still be in school?" he teased.

"I am not in school," she corrected him. "My mother forgot her dinner bucket, and I came to bring it to her."

He grinned mischievously. Ruth wasn't just pretty, she was saucy. A man didn't come across too many saucy Amish girls where he came from. Mostly, they were quiet and meek. Hannah Yoder's daughter was different, not just a pretty face and a tidy body. She had spirit, and he liked her at once. "If I thought you would bring my lunch, I might forget it, too."

Chapter Two

The hanging oil lamp cast a warm golden light over the Yoder kitchen as Ruth's family prepared for supper that evening. This was her favorite part of the day, and despite the near-tragedy of the fire, she found sweet comfort in the familiar odors of baking bread and the clatter of dishes and silverware.

Dutifully, Ruth helped her sisters carry food to the old trencher table that Dat's great-grandfather had crafted. The kitchen was Plain, spacious and as neat as the starched white *Kapp* Mam wore to Sunday services under her black bonnet.

Ruth was carrying two steaming bowls of corn chowder to the table when she heard a knock on the back door.

"Whoever could that be?" Mam asked.

Anna placed an iron skillet of fresh-baked biscuits on top of the stove. "I'll get it."

Ruth had a strange feeling she knew who the unexpected visitor was, and she hurried to the window over the sink and tugged back the corner of the yellow chintz curtain. The minute she saw him, she dropped the curtain and spun around, leaning against the sink. "Don't answer it!" she called, panic fluttering in her chest.

"Don't answer it?" Anna laughed as she walked toward the back door. "Ruth, what's gotten into you? You hit your head when that boy rolled you around in the grass today?"

Susanna giggled and covered her mouth with a chubby hand. Nothing was said or went on in Susanna's presence that wasn't repeated later to anyone who would listen.

"No, I didn't hit my head," Ruth whispered loudly. She felt silly and shaky at the same time, as if she'd played ring-around-the-rosy too long with her nephew. "It's supper time. Just let him go."

"Him?" Anna raised a blond eyebrow and Susanna giggled again.

Eli heard the sound of feminine voices on the other side of the door and yanked his straw hat off. Then, feeling silly, he dropped it back on his head. What was he doing? He wasn't *courting* the girl; he'd just stopped by after work to check on her. Okay, so it wasn't on his way home, but it *was* the proper thing to do, wasn't it? To check on a girl after she'd nearly caught her clothes on fire?

Eli groaned. Who was he kidding? He knew very well Ruth was fine. She'd made that quite clear at the school yard. He should never have come to the Yoder house. When he had left Belleville, he'd sworn off pretty girls. They were nothing but trouble. Trouble, that was what it was that had led him here tonight, and if he had any sense at all, he'd turn and run before the door opened.

That was the smart thing to do. Eli took a step back, cramming his hat down farther on his head. A smart man would run.

He was just turning away when he heard the doorknob, and he spun back, yanking off his hat again. In his mind, he already saw Ruth, pretty as a picture, smiling up at him, thanking him for rescuing her from certain death today. He smiled as the door opened.

But it wasn't Ruth, and he took a step back in surprise, nearly tripping down the step. Definitely not Ruth. This girl was taller and far rounder and not nearly so gentle on the eyes....

She looked as startled as he felt.

"H-hi." Her round cheeks reddened as she wiped her hands on her apron, a smile rising on the corners of her lips.

He had that kind of effect on girls. They smiled a lot, giggled when they looked at him. "H-hi," he echoed, feeling completely ridiculous. He heard someone whisper loudly from inside.

"Tell him I'm not here."

The girl at the door smiled more broadly, bringing dimples to her cheeks, and she took a step toward him, practically filling the doorway so he couldn't see inside.

Eli took another step back. That had to be Ruth he'd heard. It had sounded like her.

"Bet you're Eli," the girl said, crossing her arms over her plump chest.

He nodded, wishing more with every second that he'd taken that opportunity to run. "Yeah, yeah, I am." He looked down at his scuffed boots, then up at her again. "I...stopped by on my way home just to see...to make sure Ruth was all right," he stammered, and then started again. "You know, with the fire and all."

"Just on your way home from the chair shop?" She nodded, still smiling. She knew very well his uncle's farm wasn't on his way home.

He didn't know what to say, but that didn't seem to bother her.

"I'm Anna, Ruth's sister." The big girl glanced over her

shoulder. "We're just sitting down to supper. Would you like to come in? We've got plenty."

"Anna!" came Ruth's voice from inside, followed by more giggles.

For a second Eli was tempted. The smell of fresh biscuits made his stomach growl. Supper with Ruth would make the day just about perfect.

But she was a pretty girl, and he was supposed to be staying away from pretty girls.

"No. Thank you." He took another step back, making sure he hit the step. "I need to get home. Aunt Fannie will be expecting me. I just wanted to check to be sure she was okay. Ruth." Somehow his hat had gotten in his hand again, and he gestured lamely toward the house.

"She's fine," Anna said sweetly. "She really appreciates you putting the fire out on her apron and saving her from burning to death in front of all the children."

"Anna, please!" Ruth groaned from behind the door.

Eli had to suppress a grin. "Well, good night."

"Good night." Anna waved.

Eli nodded, stuck his hat back on his head, turned and made a hasty retreat before he got himself into any more trouble.

The minute Anna shut the door, Ruth grabbed her arm. "What are you doing inviting him to supper?" she whispered, not wanting Mam to hear her. In the Yoder household, there was always room for another at the table.

"He's very cute," Anna said. "He was just checking on you. He wanted to make sure you were all right." She grabbed the biscuits to put on the table. "I think he likes you. Susanna said she thought he liked you."

Ruth's heart was still fluttering in her chest. The idea of a boy that good-looking liking her was certainly not a possibility. Boys like Eli liked girls like her sister Leah.

Beautiful girls. Or they liked exciting girls like Miriam. Ruth knew she was attractive enough, but she was the steady girl, the good girl. She wasn't beautiful or exciting.

"Supper time," Mam called with authority, looking from Anna to Ruth.

Mam never missed a thing, but luckily, she said nothing about Eli being at the door. Ruth didn't want to talk about Eli. Not ever. She just wanted to pretend the whole thing with her apron catching fire had never happened. It was too embarrassing.

"I hope there's enough here," Anna said, when they'd finished silent grace.

"This is plenty, daughter."

"It all looks delicious, Anna," Ruth said, finding her normal voice. Seated here at the table with her family, she could push thoughts of Eli Lapp and all her tumbling emotions out of her head. "But then everything you make is delicious."

Anna smiled, always grateful for a compliment. Cooking seemed to be what she lived for. Ruth cared deeply for Anna, but even a sister's loving eye couldn't deny the truth that Anna's features were as ordinary as oatmeal. Her mouth was too wide, and her round cheeks as rosy as pickled beets. Anna was what Mam called a healthy girl, tall and sturdy with dimpled elbows and wide feet. The truth was, Anna took up twice the room in the buggy as her twin Miriam.

Ruth knew the neighbors whispered that Anna would never marry but would be the daughter to stay home and care for her mother in her old age, but she thought they were wrong. Surely there was a good man somewhere out there who would appreciate Anna for who she was and what she had to offer.

"That was Eli Lapp at the door just wanting to make

sure Ruth was all right. He was on his way home from the chair shop." Anna cut her gaze at Ruth.

Miriam nearly choked on her chowder. "That was Eli Lapp from Belleville at the door?" She looked at their mother. "Dorcas said he rides a Harley-Davidson motorcycle. Aunt Martha saw him."

"He's allowed to if he hasn't joined the church yet," Anna offered. "Dinah said he's *rumspringa.* You know those Pennsylvania Amish are a lot more liberal with their young people than our church."

Susanna's eyes widened. *"Rump-spinga?* What's that?"

"Rumspringa," Mam corrected gently. "Some Amish churches allow their teenage boys and girls a few years of freedom to experiment with worldly ways before they commit their lives to God. Anna is right. So long as Eli hasn't yet been baptized, he can do what he wants, within reason."

"Rumspringa," Susanna repeated.

"He's wild is what he is." Miriam's eyes twinkled with mischief. "That's what everyone is saying. Handsome and wild."

Ruth's throat tightened. She was just starting to feel calmer, and now here they were talking about that boy again. It was almost as bad as having him right here at the supper table! Why was Miriam teasing her like this? She knew very well Ruth wasn't interested in Eli Lapp…not in any boy.

"Let us eat before everything is cold." Mam didn't raise her voice, but she didn't have to. All eyes turned to their plates, and for several loud ticks of the mantel clock, there was no sound but the clink of forks and spoons against Mam's blue-and-white ironstone plates and the loud purring of Susanna's tabby cat under the table.

They were just clearing away the dishes when a knock came at the kitchen door. "Who can that be now?" Miriam asked. "Think it's Eli Lapp again?"

Anna and Miriam exchanged glances and giggled. Ruth stepped into the hall, seriously considering marching straight up the stairs to an early bedtime.

"I'll get it." Anna bustled for the door.

"*Ne.* I'll get it." Mam straightened her *Kapp* before answering the door.

When Ruth peeked around the corner, she was relieved to see that it was Samuel Mast, their neighbor.

He plucked at his well-trimmed beard as he stepped into the kitchen. "You're eating. I should have waited."

"*Ne, ne,*" Mam said. "You come in and have coffee and Anna's rhubarb pudding with us. You know you are always welcome. Did Roman say how much the repairs on the school would cost?"

Anna carried a steaming mug of coffee to Dat's place. Since Dat's death, the seat was always reserved for company, and Samuel often filled it.

Ruth thought Samuel was sweet on Mam, but her mother would certainly deny it. Samuel was a God-fearing man with a big farm and a prize herd of milk cows; he was also eight years younger than Mam. Nevertheless, Ruth observed, he came often and stayed late, whenever someone could watch his children for the evening.

Samuel was a widower and Mam a widow. With Dat two years in the grave and Samuel's wife nearly four, it was time they both remarried. Everyone said so. But Ruth didn't believe her mother was ready to take that step, not even for solid and hardworking Samuel.

The trouble was, Ruth thought, Mam couldn't discourage Samuel's visits without hurting his feelings. They all valued his friendship. He was a deacon in their church, not a bishop, as Dat had been, but a respected and good man. Everyone liked him. Ruth liked him, just not as a replacement for her father.

And now Samuel would be here all evening again, delaying Ruth's plans for a serious conversation with Mam about Irwin Beachy running from the fire. She didn't want to make accusations without proof, but she couldn't keep this from her mother. If Irwin *had* started the blaze, something would have to be done. But now there would be no chance to get Mam alone before bedtime. Samuel had settled in Dat's chair, where he would stay until the clock struck eleven and Mam began pulling down the window shades. Talking to her mother about Irwin would have to wait until tomorrow.

Maybe that was a better idea anyway. Ruth was still flustered. First the incident at the school with that Eli, and then him showing up at their door asking for her. This had been a terrible day, and that wild Pennsylvania boy hadn't made it any better.

Every Friday, three of the Yoder girls took butter, eggs, flowers and seasonal produce to Spence's Auction and Bazaar in Dover, where they rented a table and sold their wares to the English. They would rise early so that they could set up their stand before the first shoppers of the day came to buy food from the Amish Market and prowl through the aisles of antiques, vegetables and yard sale junk. If the girls were lucky, they would sell out before noon.

The income was important to the household. There were items that they needed that Mam's salary couldn't cover. And no matter how tight the budget, each girl who worked was allowed to take a portion of the profit for her marriage savings or to buy something that she wanted.

The sisters shared equally with Susanna, who always did her best to help.

Susanna loved the auction. She liked to watch the English tourists and she loved to poke through the dusty tables of glass dogs and plastic toys in the flea market. Today, Susanna had made a real find, an old Amish-style rag doll without a face. The doll had obviously had many adventures. Somewhere she'd lost her *Kapp* and apron, but Ruth promised that she would sew Dolly a new wardrobe and assured her sister that this doll was Plain enough to please even the bishop.

Today had been a slow day. They hadn't sold everything, and it was long past lunchtime. Now it was clouding up in the west, and it looked to Ruth as if they might get an afternoon thunderstorm.

Across the way, Aunt Martha and Cousin Dorcas were already packing up their baked-goods stall. Ruth was just about to suggest to Miriam that they leave when, suddenly, there was a loud rumble.

Heads whipped around as Eli Lapp came roaring down the driveway between the lines of stalls on a battered old motorbike. Ruth almost laughed in spite of herself at the sight of him on the rickety contraption. Even she could see that it was no Harley motorcycle, as Aunt Martha had claimed. It was an ancient motorized scooter, hand-painted in awful shades of yellow, lime and black.

Susanna's mouth opened in a wide *O* as she pointed at the motor scooter. Miriam called out and waved, and to Ruth's horror, the Belleville boy braked his machine right in front of the Yoder stall.

"Hey!" he shouted, over the clatter of the bike. "Ruth, good to see you again."

Ruth's eyes narrowed as she felt a wash of hot blood rise up from her throat to scald her cheeks. Aunt Martha and

Dorcas were staring from their stall. Even the English were chuckling and ogling them. Or maybe they were looking at the ugly bike; she couldn't tell.

"Want a ride?" Eli dared, grinning at Ruth.

She was mortified by the attention. Eli Lapp was not only riding a ridiculous motor scooter, he wasn't dressed Plain. He was wearing motorcycle boots, tight Englisher blue jeans and a blue-and-white T-shirt, two sizes too small, that read "Nittany Lions."

"Ne. I do not want a ride," she retorted. "Go away." She thought she spoke with authority, but her voice came out choked and squeaky, and Miriam giggled.

"It's perfectly safe, teacher's girl," he said. "I've even got a helmet." He held up a red one, almost as battered as the bike.

"Ne," Ruth repeated firmly, avoiding eye contact, even though he was staring right at her.

"If you won't, I will," Miriam cried, throwing up both hands.

And before Ruth could utter more than a feeble *"Ne,"* her sister scrambled around the table, hitched up her skirt and apron, and jumped on the back of the scooter.

"I want a ride, too!" Susanna declared, bouncing up and down.

Ruth cut her gaze to Miriam as she watched her boldly wrap her arms around Eli's waist. "Miriam," she ordered, "get off—"

Eli winked at Ruth, and the motorbike took off down the drive, out of the auction and onto the street, leaving her standing there looking foolish and Susanna jumping up and down for joy.

"Oh! Oh!" Susanna clapped her hands. "Did you see Miriam ride?"

"Help me load the rest of our things into the buggy. She'll be back in a minute," Ruth said, a lump in her throat.

She told herself she was upset that Miriam was doing something she shouldn't be, but she knew in her heart of hearts it was that boy again. He was making her feel this way. And she didn't like it. Not one bit.

As Ruth walked to the buggy, trying to look casual, she glanced in her aunt's direction. Aunt Martha had her head close together with Dorcas, and the two were talking excitedly. That was definitely not good. Miriam's poor decision would be all over Kent County by supper time. And there would be no doubt who would be held accountable.

Ruth would.

She was the oldest left at home. Susanna and Miriam were her responsibility. They had not been baptized into the church yet, but she had. She should have known better than to let Miriam do something so foolish, so not Plain.

Ruth was just checking the horse's harness when she heard the growl of the motorbike as it grew closer again. Stroking the old mare's broad neck, she turned to see Eli and Miriam riding straight at her. A moment later, her sister was holding three ice-cream cones in the air and trying to get off the scooter without showing too much bare leg. Eli was laughing and talking to her as if they were old friends.

"He bought us ice cream." Miriam licked a big drip of chocolate off her cone and handed the vanilla one to Susanna. "What do you say, Susanna?"

"Danke," Susanna chirped.

"And here's one for you." Miriam had a twinkle in her eye as she held out the ice cream to Ruth. "I know you like strawberry."

"No, thank you," Ruth said stiffly. "I don't want any."

Miriam shoved the cone into her hand. "Don't be such

a prune," she whispered. "Eat it. Mam wouldn't want you to waste food."

Ruth glared at Eli as she felt the cold cream run down her fingers.

"I see Miriam got back in one piece," Dorcas called as she hurried across the driveway toward Ruth. "Mam saw her and—"

"Here." Flustered, Ruth handed her cousin the ice-cream cone. "You like ice cream. You eat it."

Eli looked right at Ruth, laughed and roared away on his noisy machine.

Chapter Three

Ruth glanced at Mam and then turned her attention back to Blackie, their driving gelding, and eased him onto the shoulder of the busy road to allow a line of cars to pass. Blackie was a young horse, and Ruth didn't completely trust him yet, not like she did old Molly, so she liked to keep a sharp eye out for traffic.

"So why did you wait so long to tell me about Irwin?" Her mother's soft voice carried easily over the regular clip-clop of Blackie's hooves on the road and the rumble of the buggy wheels. The rain, which had held off all day, was coming down in a spattering of large drops.

Miriam had gone ahead with Anna, Susanna and Johanna and her children to the quilting frolic at Lydia Beachy's house in the big buggy, leaving her and Mam to follow in the smaller courting buggy. Dat had brought this single-seat carriage from Pennsylvania with him twenty-six years ago. It was just the right size for two, perfect for private conversation. Ruth had counted on being able to voice her concerns about Irwin, and she wanted to tell Mam about this afternoon's incident with Eli Lapp and his ridiculous motorbike before anyone else did.

"Ruth?" Mam pressed.

"I meant to, but…" An ominous roll of thunder sounded off to the west, and she flicked the reins to urge Blackie into a trot as she pulled back onto the road. "But Samuel came last night and then there was no chance to talk with you alone and today we were both gone all day."

"I see. Well, Irwin wasn't in school today."

"He wasn't?"

"I asked three of Irwin's cousins why he wasn't there and got three different excuses," Mam said.

Ruth sighed. "I don't want to accuse him. I just thought it was strange that he'd run away like that. I suppose he could have seen the fire and been trying to put it out." She hesitated. "But since Irwin is always making mischief…"

"Losing his whole family in a fire, coming to Delaware to live with people he hardly knows, it's no wonder he acts out." Mam folded her arms in a gesture that meant no nonsense. "I won't judge him until we know the truth, and neither should you."

Ruth didn't want to argue with Mam, but neither was she going to hold her tongue when she had something to say. "He did set Samuel's outhouse on fire last month. He gave Toby a black eye and you sent him home twice from school for fighting this month."

Mam frowned. "The boy has a lot of anger inside. He needs love, not accusations and false judgments."

"But if he makes a habit of playing with matches…"

"Where's your charity? In my experience, the wildest boys turn out to be the most dependable men."

Ruth winced. "You know I don't mean to be uncharitable. I just thought you should know what I saw with my own eyes."

"And rightly so." Mam nodded. "Now that I do know, I'll handle it."

When Ruth didn't comment, Mam continued. "The

school can be repaired, but if people start talking about Irwin, the damage to a child's soul may not be so easy to mend."

"You're right, but what if he's a danger to others?"

"Have faith, Ruth. I'll do my part, the Beachys will do theirs, and God will do the rest."

"What will you do?" Her heart went out to the boy, as unlikable as he was, but they had to think of the other children's safety, too. As much as she valued her mother's judgment, she had to be satisfied that they weren't taking unnecessary chances to protect Irwin.

"I'll talk to him privately." Mam pursed her mouth. "Last night, Samuel confided that he suspects his twins know something about the fire, something they were afraid to tell."

"What made him think that?"

"Samuel said it wasn't what they said—it was what they *didn't* say." Mam squeezed her hand. "We'll get to the bottom of this. Not to worry."

She glanced at her mother, wanting to believe her, wishing her own faith in others came as easily as it seemed to come to Mam. "You always say that."

"And it's always true, isn't it? Things usually work out for the best."

Her mother smiled at her, and Ruth was struck by how young and pretty she still was at forty-six. Tonight, she was wearing a lavender dress with her black apron, and her black bonnet was tied over her starched white *Kapp*. No one would guess by looking at Mam's waistline that she'd given birth to seven children. "You must have been a beautiful bride, Mam."

"Why, Ruth Yoder, what a thing to say. I hope I was properly Plain. Vanity is not a trait to be encouraged."

Ruth suppressed a smile. Mam might not admit it, but

she cared about her appearance. It was Ruth's opinion that on her wedding day, her mother must have been just as beautiful as Leah. Hadn't Dat always said he'd snapped up the prettiest girl in Kent County? "No one could accuse you of *Hochmut*, Mam. You never show a speck of self-pride."

"Not according to your *grossmama*. It took a long time for your dat's mother and family to accept me after we married."

"Because you grew up Mennonite and had to join the Amish Church to marry Dat?" That was something of a family scandal, but once she had joined the church, no one now could ever accuse Mam of not being properly Plain in her demeanor or her faith.

"Maybe, or maybe it was that your dat was her only son."

"And we were all girls."

"God's gifts to us, every one of you." Mam squeezed her hand. "Believe that, Ruth. Your father never blamed me that we had no sons. He always said he got exactly what he prayed for."

Ruth's throat constricted as she turned Blackie onto Norman and Lydia Beachy's long dirt lane behind the Troyer buggy. "I miss Dat."

"And so do I. Every day."

"Does that mean you're not going to marry Samuel?"

Hannah chuckled. "If I were to consider such a thing, wouldn't it be wiser to settle that matter with Samuel first?" She patted Ruth's hand again. "Mind your own mending, daughter."

As Blackie's quick trot drew the buggy toward the house and barn, Ruth realized that she hadn't had time to tell Mam about Miriam's ride on the back of Eli Lapp's motor scooter.

As the buggy neared the rambling two-story farmhouse, Ruth saw several of the Beachy children in the yard taking charge of the guests' horses. As she reined in Blackie, she spotted Irwin coming out from behind a corncrib to take hold of the horse's bridle. "A good evening to you," she called.

Irwin winced and took a firmer grip on Blackie. The horse twitched his ears.

"We missed you at school today, Irwin," Mam said mildly.

He mumbled something, fixing his gaze on his bare feet.

Ruth climbed down out of the buggy and gathered their quilting supplies. "Did you hurt yourself?" she asked, noticing a soiled bandage on the boy's left hand.

"Ne." He tucked his hand behind his back.

"It's all right, dear." Mam smiled at him as she picked up the *Blitzkuchen* Anna had baked. "No need to explain. I'll talk to Lydia about it."

His eyes widened in alarm. "Don't do that, teacher."

"Then we'd best have a private talk. Come in early tomorrow morning."

"But that's Saturday. There's no school on Saturday."

"I need help to move some of the desks around to make room for Roman to do the repairs." She paused. "And, Irwin? Don't be late."

"Be careful with Blackie," Ruth cautioned. "He's easily spooked."

Irwin nodded. *"Ya,* I will." He led the horse a few steps, then glanced back over his shoulder. "You won't say nothin' to Cousin Lydia, will ya?"

"After we have our talk, I'll decide if there's anything Lydia and Norman need to know."

"I don't mean to make trouble." He shrugged. "It just happens."

"Sometimes trouble finds us all," Mam said as she started up the steps to the house. Ruth hurried ahead and opened the door for her.

Inside Lydia's kitchen, Hannah and Ruth greeted several neighbors. From the next room, where everyone had gathered, Ruth could hear the excited buzz of voices as members of the community caught up on the latest news. One of Lydia's girls took their black bonnets and capes, and Lydia turned from the stove to welcome them.

Lydia was a tall, thin, freckle-faced woman with a narrow beak of a nose, a wide mouth and very little chin. "I'm so glad you could all come," she said with genuine warmth, deftly sliding a pan of hot gingerbread onto the counter. Lydia's voice came out flat, evidence of her midwestern upbringing. "After yesterday's fire, I didn't know if you'd feel up to joining us."

Ruth couldn't help noting Lydia's rounded tummy. Another baby on the way. God was certainly blessing the Beachy family. Lydia was a true inspiration to Ruth. She hadn't hesitated when Irwin's family had been lost, and she had welcomed him into her family.

"It smells wonderful in here," Mam said, glancing around at the pies and cakes set on the table and counters. "You know we wouldn't miss your frolic. The quilt money will help with the school repairs."

Ruth looked around for her sister Johanna. The community quilting project to support the school was her idea. Johanna had sketched antique quilt patterns and carefully chosen the fabrics and colors. Everyone contributed to the cost of the material, and at each quilting night, every woman would sew one or more squares. Later this summer, they would assemble them in a daylong effort.

Ruth wasn't nearly as talented with a needle as Johanna, but she loved the chance to get together with friends and neighbors, especially when they were all working for such a good cause.

Lydia's crowded kitchen, smelling strongly of cinnamon, ginger and pine oil, was pandemonium as always. Both the woodstove and the gas stove were lit, and the room was overwarm. A large, shallow pan of milk, covered with a thin layer of cheesecloth, sat waiting for the cream to rise beside a spotless glass butter churn. On the counter and in the big soapstone sink, the last of the Beachy supper dishes stood, waiting to be washed. Without being asked, Ruth rolled up her sleeves, took down a work apron from a hook and went to the sink.

Four small giggling children, one of them Johanna's three-year-old son Jonah, darted around the long wooden table chasing an orange tabby. The cat leaped to a counter and dashed to safety, barely missing a lemon pie piled high with meringue, and headed for a direct collision with the unprotected pan of milk.

Lydia juggled a pitcher of lemonade in one hand as she snagged the cat with the other. Without hesitation, she then separated two toddlers tugging on the same stuffed toy. "Out," she commanded, shooing the children toward the sitting room. As the last little girl's bonnet strings passed through the doorway, Lydia turned to Mam with a look of despair.

"A long day?" Mam asked.

"I hate to complain, Hannah."

"Complaining is not the same as sharing our woes."

"It's that boy. I'm at my wits' end with Irwin. I try to be patient, but—"

Ruth turned back to the sink full of dishes and tried to

give them a little privacy even though her mother and Lydia were only a few feet away.

"I know he's having a hard time adjusting, Lydia," Mam supplied.

"He is. He and our Vernon scrap like cats in a barrel. At twelve, the boy should have some sense, but…"

"He'll come around," Mam soothed.

Lydia lowered her voice. "It's what I tell Norman, but he says we can't trust the boy. I didn't think it would be this hard."

"No one doubts that you and Norman have been good to Irwin."

"We try, but he's late for meals. Remiss in his chores. He let the dairy cows into the orchard twice." Lydia sighed. "I hope we haven't made a mistake in opening our home—"

A baby's wail cut through the murmur of female voices from the other room. "Is that your little Henry?" Mam asked.

"Go, get off your feet and see to him, Lydia," Ruth said, turning from the sink. "You, too, Mam. I can finish up here." The dishes clean and stacked neatly in a wooden drying rack, she dried her hands on a towel. She was just reaching for the can of coffee when she heard her aunt Martha's strident voice.

"Hannah, here you are." She bustled into the room, letting Lydia pass, but blocking Mam. "I wondered where you were."

Ruth forced a polite greeting. Aunt Martha was more trouble than a headache. According to Dat, his older sister's hair had once been as red as his. Now the wisps of hair showing under her *Kapp* were gray, and the only auburn hairs were two curling ones sprouting on her chin. She was a tall, sparse woman with a thin mouth and a voice that could saw lumber.

"How are the children?" Mam asked. "And Reuben? Is he well?"

"His bad knee is troubling him. He thinks we might have rain all weekend. I left him working on his sermon for Sunday services."

"I'm sure it will be as good as his last service," Ruth said, unable to help herself. Reuben was a good man, but he could be long-winded. *Very* long-winded. In fact, he could speak more and say less than anyone she knew.

Mam threw Ruth a warning look, and Ruth hid a smile.

Aunt Martha glanced around, a sure sign that she was about to launch into one of her reprimands. When she did that, Ruth could never be sure if she was looking to be sure no one was near, or hoping they were.

"I've been wanting to speak to you, Hannah."

She took on a tone Ruth knew well. Mam was in for it.

"You were my younger brother's wife, and I have a duty to tell you when I see something not right." Aunt Martha cleared her throat. "You, too, Ruth."

Ruth steeled herself. So she was in for it as well.

Aunt Martha was a faithful member of the church and the community, but she liked to point out the errors of other people, especially Mam's daughters. And too often, she saw a small sin bigger than it actually was.

Ruth wasn't sure if she was in the mood tonight to be too charitable. "Aunt Martha…"

"Quiet, girl. Show some respect for your elders. It's for your own good and your mother's. I don't say this lightly." She sucked in her cheeks in disapproval.

Ruth gritted her teeth. She had to learn to be more

patient. Like Mam. She wanted to be more patient; it was just that sometimes Aunt Martha made it difficult.

"And me being the wife of the minister, well, that makes it my duty, as well…" Martha took a deep breath and pointed a plump finger at Mam. "Hannah, your household is out of control." She scowled at Ruth. "And you're partly to blame."

Ruth bit her bottom lip to keep from speaking up. It did no good with Aunt Martha, not when she was like this. It was better just to keep quiet, listen and hope the tirade passed quickly.

"And I'm not the only one to have noticed," Martha went on. "Reuben was just saying to me the other day that it's unseemly for you, Hannah, to be teaching school like an unmarried girl."

"I'm sorry my teaching troubles you," Mam said. "But our school needs a teacher, and I'm qualified."

"The school board and the bishop approved Mam's appointment," Ruth put in. "And her salary helps to support our family."

Martha frowned. "Your mother should have remarried by now. Then it wouldn't be necessary for her to work."

"It's only been two years, Martha. Jonas…"

"Two years and seven months, sister. By custom, it's time you put away your mourning and accepted another husband. If you had a God-fearing man in your house, your girls wouldn't be acting inappropriately."

"Inappropriately?" Mam's brows arched. "How have they behaved inappropriately? Lately?" she clarified, spunk in her voice.

"Today. At Spence's."

"Eli Lapp was there," Ruth explained quickly. "He bought ice cream for Susanna and Miriam."

Aunt Martha eyes widened with great exaggeration. "So

this is the first you've heard of it, Hannah? Miriam made
a show of herself with that wild Belleville boy. She rode
on his motorcycle in front of everyone. With her skirts up
and her *Kapp* flying off her head. Her arms were around
his waist. I saw it with my own eyes."

"Really?" Mam asked.

Ruth noticed Lydia and Aunt Martha's younger sister,
Aunt Alma, peering into the kitchen. Lydia's cheeks took
on a rosy hue. "I'm sorry. We didn't mean to—"

"Ne," Mam said. "There's nothing to hide. Martha was
telling me that my tomboy daughter was riding behind
Roman's nephew on a motorcycle at Spence's today."

"Scooter," Ruth corrected gently, feeling she had to
defend her sister, even though she didn't really want to
defend Eli. "It wasn't really a motorcycle. It was a motor
scooter—"

"Scooter? Cycle? It doesn't matter what the loud English
machine is called," Aunt Martha declared. "It's unseemly
for a young girl like my niece to make such a spectacle
of herself." She glared at Ruth. "Or for her older sister to
allow it."

Mam chuckled. "It would be just like Miriam to take
a ride on the machine, wouldn't it?" She shook her head.
"But it's not so bad, is it? She's not joined the church yet.
It's natural for her to dabble with the world…just as *we*
did once." A smile tugged at the corners of her mouth as
if she knew some secret about Aunt Martha that Ruth and
the others didn't.

"It's wrong," Aunt Martha argued, her cheeks turning
red. "You've been far too lenient with your daughters."

"Mam is a good mother and a good role model," Ruth
said.

"You hold your tongue, young woman," Aunt Martha

fussed. "This would never have happened if my brother was alive."

"*Ne*. Probably not," Mam said. "And I agree that a motor scooter is dangerous, especially without a helmet. I'll speak with Miriam about it."

"You don't understand the danger of situations like these," Aunt Martha went on. "Of what people will say. How could you? You weren't born Plain."

"What does Mam being born Mennonite have to do with—"

Mam silenced Ruth with a wave of her hand. Once Mam's temper was set off, she could handle Aunt Martha, and Mam's amusement had definitely faded.

"Martha, you should mind the sharpness of your tongue. I don't think my being born Mennonite has anything to do with my daughter taking a ride on an old motorbike, and I don't think your brother, my husband, would approve of such talk. None of us should be too quick to pass judgment on Eli Lapp. He's *rumspringa* and a visitor among us. How can we condemn what his church and family allows?"

"I suppose you believe Ruth is right, too." Martha planted her hands on her broad hips. "In allowing Miriam to do such a thing."

"Ruth is a sensible girl," Hannah pointed out. "She'd never let her sisters come to harm. I trust her judgment."

"Maybe you shouldn't this time." Aunt Alma, a shorter and paler reflection of Aunt Martha, hustled up to stand beside her sister. "I had a letter just yesterday from our cousin in Belleville about this Lapp boy. It's worse than we first thought."

"Tell them, Alma. I think it's for the best we all know what's what," Aunt Martha prodded.

Aunt Alma needed no further encouragement. "Rumor

has it that Eli's family sent him away because he got a girl in the family way and refused to marry her."

Ruth's chest tightened, and she suddenly felt sick to her stomach. She didn't want hear any more, but she couldn't help herself. She couldn't walk away.

"So!" Aunt Martha cried, seeming almost pleased with the awful accusation. "Is that the kind of young man we want to welcome into our community?"

Eli moved deeper into the shadows of the lilac bush that grew outside the Beachys' kitchen window. He could see Ruth standing very still near the sink, a drying towel in her slender hands. There were other women in the room, but Eli paid no attention to them; he saw no one but Ruth. Light from a kerosene lantern illuminated the planes of her heart-shaped face and glinted off the strands of red-gold hair that escaped from her *Kapp*. She was a beautiful girl. No, a beautiful woman.

He wished he'd gotten here sooner, wished he'd thought sooner of bringing the hand drill that Roman had promised to loan Norman. If he'd walked faster across the fields, maybe he would have had been in the yard in time to take Ruth's horse when she and her family had arrived. Then he would have had the opportunity to speak a few words with her.

It was obvious that Ruth Yoder didn't think too much of him, which was a new experience for him. Back home, girls and their mothers and their aunties usually liked him a lot, sometimes too much. He supposed it was his bad luck to be born with his dat's features. Too pretty for a man, they'd always called him, too fair of face to be properly Plain. Truth was, Dat's face had gotten him in plenty of trouble…as it had his son.

This was one time Eli would have liked his looks to

be an asset. He'd taken one look at that mane of tumbled auburn hair in the school yard, and his heart had swelled in his chest, beating as if he'd run a mile. There was something about Ruth Yoder, something about the curve of her lips and her stubborn little chin that got to him in a way no other girl had ever done.

But Ruth Yoder was a religious girl, the kind he'd always steered clear of, the kind of girl he knew would have no interest in him. So why had he walked two miles through the rain tonight to catch sight of her?

As much as he hated to admit it, he knew the answer. He'd been lightning-struck by a red-headed girl with soot on her nose and fire in her eyes.

Chapter Four

More white *Kapps* and curious faces appeared in the archway leading to the sitting room. The women all stared at Ruth, her mother, Aunt Martha and Aunt Alma. Fortunately, Lydia came to the rescue. Bouncing a wailing infant on her shoulder, she pushed through the crowd and raised her strident voice above little Henry's cries. "Shouldn't we get to work on the quilt?"

"*Ya,*" Mam agreed, nodding. "We have much to do." She linked her arm through Aunt Martha's. "Come, sit by me, sister. Your stitches are so neat that I find myself inspired just watching you."

Aunt Martha's beady eyes narrowed in suspicion, but Mam's genuine smile weakened her fortitude. "All right, if you want. I never meant harm, you know, Hannah. We have to look out for each other."

Aunt Alma nodded vigorously. "*Ya,* we must. You are our dear brother's wife."

"It is hard to be a mother," Aunt Martha added. "Harder still to be a mother without the strong guidance of a husband."

Several others agreed and apprehensive expressions gave way to general good humor. Whatever the women had heard would soon make the rounds, but Ruth knew that her mother was liked and appreciated in the community. Mam would not come out the worst in this.

"Ruth, could you pull the kitchen shades for me?"

Johanna, who'd come into the kitchen as the others were filing into the sitting room, winked at Ruth as she crossed to the window to help. "What was that all about?" she whispered. "What's Miriam done now?"

Ruth bit back a chuckle. "I'm in hot water, too. And Mam."

Her sister made a tsk-tsk sound with her tongue and both broke into suppressed giggles. "For shame," Johanna admonished.

"Johanna!" Lydia called from the next room. "We can't start until you assign squares."

"Go on," Ruth urged. "I'll get the shades."

As Johanna left the room, Ruth turned back to the bank of windows that lined the wall, assuring plenty of light in the big kitchen even in winter. No curtains covered the wide glass panes, just spartan white shades. There was nothing to hide, but drawing the shades after dark was a custom strictly held to in the Amish community.

As Ruth reached for the last blind, she noticed movement near Lydia's lilac bushes outside the window. At first, she assumed it must be one of the children. But the figure was too tall and broad-shouldered to be a child. She paused, drawing close to the window for a better look, cupping her hands around her eyes to cut down on the glare reflected from light inside the kitchen.

To her surprise, a man stepped out from behind the lilacs almost directly in front of her. Light from the window shone on his face as he turned toward her, and she realized she was almost nose to nose with Eli Lapp.

Ruth jerked back, heart pounding as though she'd been

racing Miriam to the orchard. What was he doing there, spying on the women? Was he some kind of pervert? She grabbed hold of the shade and yanked it down, but not before she caught a glimpse of his expression. He was grinning at her!

Cheeks burning, she marched across the kitchen and flung open the back door. "What are you doing out here?" she demanded.

"Watching you."

"Where are your manners?" She ran her hand over her *Kapp* and then dropped it to her side, once again flustered by him. She'd caught him doing something wrong; why was she the one who felt foolish? "Did your mother never teach you better?" she demanded, trying to cover the awkwardness she felt with anger. "Why would you stare at me through a window?"

"You're pretty when you're cross. Did you know that?"

"You! You are impossible!"

"You should have talked to me when I came to your house," he said, still grinning like a mule. "I just wanted to know if you were all right."

"I'm fine. I told you that at the school. I'm not hurt." She paused to catch her breath. "I thank you for checking on me, but—"

"How many sisters do you have?"

"How many sisters?" she repeated. She felt tongue-tied, awkward. She knew she must be as red as a beet. It wasn't as if she wasn't used to talking to boys. She had lots of friends who were boys: Dan, Charley, even Gideon, but none of them had ever made her so...so not like herself. "Why? Why do you ask me that?"

"Don't you know how many sisters you have? It must be a lot."

There was a broom standing beside the door. She wanted to pick it up and hit him with it. She'd never wanted to cause hurt to anyone before, but this…this Eli Lapp was impossible. She forced herself to speak calmly. "There is my older sister Johanna, the twins, Miriam and Anna. Anna met you at the door—"

"Aha. So you *were* listening. You told her to tell me to go away. You were afraid to talk to me," he said.

"I was not. I was helping my mother put supper on the table. It was not the best time for a guest to arrive uninvited. And now you know I am fine. I have thanked you." She crossed her arms over her chest. "So you can leave me alone."

Eli took a step closer. She could smell some kind of shaving lotion or maybe men's perfume. Who could tell what he would wear? What he might do? But it smelled nice. Manly. "You didn't answer my question."

There he was making her feel dizzy again. "What question?"

"How many sisters you have," he teased. "A teacher's daughter, you should be good with math."

"Don't be ridiculous! I know how many sisters I have. There are seven of us."

"All redheads? I like redheads."

Unconsciously, Ruth tucked a stray curl back under her *Kapp*. "That is none of your business. I'm going back inside, and you should go…go wherever your affairs take you." She turned away.

"Do they have names, these other sisters? Are they all as pretty as you are?"

She spun back, quickly losing control of her patience again. "There's Johanna, me, Anna, Miriam, Leah, Rebecca and Susanna. And they are all prettier than me."

"I'd have to see that to believe it."

Ruth opened her mouth, then closed it. Not knowing what else to say, she closed the door hard and hurried into the sitting room.

She found a seat between Dinah and Anna and located her own sewing kit. It seemed that everyone there was talking at once. Miriam was passing out squares of cloth, and young and old were busy threading needles.

"Dinah has suggested that we hold the end-of-year school picnic early," Mam said. "She has another idea to help pay for the building repairs."

"We could invite the other Amish churches," Dinah explained, "and have a pie auction for the men. Each unmarried woman will bake her favorite pie and donate it, and the bachelors will bid on them."

"And whoever buys a pie gets to eat lunch with the girl who made it," Johanna explained. "They do it at the Cedar Hill Church in Nebraska where Dinah's cousin lives. And they always make lots of money."

Ruth tried to look interested in the plans, but she couldn't really concentrate. She kept thinking about what Eli had said. He said she was pretty. No one had ever told her she was pretty. Did he mean it? Why did she care?

Then she thought about what Aunt Alma had said about the letter she'd received. Could it be true? Could Eli have gotten a girl in the family way? Sometimes even Plain youth strayed from Amish beliefs, but such mistakes were rare. She'd never heard of any Plain couple who'd failed to marry if there was a babe coming. If Eli had gotten a girl pregnant, he'd be married now, living in Belleville, wouldn't he?

"Ruth." Dinah nudged her and motioned to Hannah. "Your mam wants something from the carriage."

Ruth looked up.

"That old section of quilt in the black bag," Mam said.

"The one with my great-grandmother's sunflower pattern. I think we left it under the buggy seat." She glanced back at Lydia. "It's not in the best of shape, but it's so pretty, I've always kept it."

Ruth nodded and rose, then hesitated. What if Eli Lapp was still out there? She didn't want to see him. Couldn't. Not after the way he'd teased her...not after the way she'd talked to him.

But there was no way to refuse her mother, not without giving her a reason, and right now the idea of that was more frightening than the idea of coming nose to nose with Eli again.

Forcing herself to move, Ruth picked her way through the closely seated women. As she reached the door, she contemplated what she would do if Eli was still standing outside near the kitchen door. Not that she was afraid of him. She'd simply ignore him. He could grin foolishly at her if he wanted to, but if he got no reaction from her, he'd soon leave her alone. The Yoder girls didn't associate with boys like him.

Immediately, a flood of confusion washed through her. Was she as lacking in grace as Aunt Martha? Was she judging Eli and finding him guilty, simply on gossip? What if the whole story was wrong? In her eagerness to share, Aunt Alma didn't always get the details right. What if Eli was innocent of any crime other than riding an ugly motor scooter and coming to Delaware to work in his uncle's chair shop?

And he'd said she was pretty. She smiled, in spite of herself.

Her heartbeat quickened as she opened the back door and descended the wooden kitchen steps to the yard, eyeing the lilac bushes. There was no sign of Eli there. Near the barn, several small boys chased each other in a game of tag, but there was no sign of the Belleville boy there either. If she could just find her horse and the courting buggy in the dark, amid a sea of black buggies, she could grab the quilt square and hurry back into the house.

Irwin stepped out of the corncrib and walked out into the muddy yard. "Looking for your carriage?"

Irwin was very Plain, even for an Amish, so Plain that he stood out among the other boys. His trousers were too high on skinny ankles; the corners of his mouth were red and crusted, and his narrow shoulders sagged with the weight of a man six times his age. He looked as though he could do with a few good meals and a haircut.

Her mother's words about being quick to judge echoed in her ears. Was she judging both Irwin and Eli unfairly? Would she be just like her Aunt Martha in ten years?

"I did like you said," Irwin volunteered. "You said your horse was easy spooked, so I unhitched him and turned him into an empty stall in the barn. Your buggy is in the barn, too."

It was more words than she'd ever heard Irwin offer at one time. And putting Blackie in the barn was a kind thing to do. "Thank you," she said, smiling at him. Maybe Mam was right; maybe there was more to this boy than anyone saw at first glance.

He tilted his head and reverted to his usual soft stammer. "Sure," he said, then walked away.

Raindrops spattered her face and arms as she hurried to the barn. Inside, a single lantern hung from a big crossbeam. Dat's buggy was where Irwin had said it would be, standing alone in the center of the aisle between the box stalls. Blackie raised his head and nickered. Ruth went to him and rubbed his head, noting that a big bucket of fresh water hung from one corner post, and someone had tossed hay into the manger. "Good boy," she murmured.

"Me or him?"

The voice from inside the buggy startled her. Eli Lapp. *Again.*

She sucked in a breath and made an effort to hold back the sharp retort that rose to her lips. "Are you still here?" she asked, her voice far too breathy for either of them to believe she was entirely composed.

He chuckled, a deep sound of amusement that made her stomach flip over. "Maybe I hoped you'd come out here looking for me."

She stared at him. "Why would I do that?"

He grinned. "Tell the truth. You did, didn't you?"

"*Ne.* N-not for you. Mam asked me to fetch something from the carriage."

She hadn't been able to see him clearly in the shadows outside the house, but she could see him now. Eli was wearing Plain clothes tonight, black trousers, blue shirt, straw hat, but he was still *fancy.* He was chewing a piece of hay, and it gave him a rakish look.

Hochmut, she thought. But she couldn't deny that she found him handsome, so handsome that she could feel it in the pit of her stomach. Was this temptation? The kind Uncle Reuben talked about in his sermons sometimes?

"Be a shame to waste a courting buggy," he said. "A Kishacoquillas buggy, if I'm not mistaken." He offered her his hand. "Why don't you come up and tell me about it?"

She tucked her hands behind her back. "I just need the bag from under the seat. There's a piece of an old quilt in it. My sister wanted us to bring it for the pattern." Now she was rambling. She wanted to leave Mam's bag and run back to the house to the safety of the women's chatter.

"Still scared?" He was teasing her again.

"Of what?"

"Me?" He held out his hand seeming to dare her.

She would not get into the buggy with him. It was a bad idea, a decision that could only... But somehow, without realizing how or why, she found herself clasping his hand. It was warm and calloused, a strong hand, and nothing at all like the familiar hands of her sisters.

The next thing she knew, she was perched on the seat beside him.

"See," he said, grinning at her. "I come in peace."

"You...you," she sputtered. "I don't like you one bit."

He laughed. "Oh, yes, you do. Otherwise you wouldn't have come looking for me. Or gotten into the buggy." He looked down. "And you wouldn't still be holding my hand."

Ruth jerked her hand from his, mortified. It wasn't that she meant to let him hold her hand; he just had her so confused.

She fumbled under the seat for Mam's bag. Eli's all-too-warm leg rested innocently against hers, making her vividly aware of his strong body and broad shoulders. He smelled clean and all male. She'd always hated the stench of tobacco that clung to some men, but there was none of that about Eli. His hair and body were fresh, his old high-tops were polished to a shine, and the nails on his big hands were clean and cut straight across.

"I have to go back inside."

"*Ya*, I suppose you do," he agreed. "But it's nice sitting here, don't you think?"

"*Ne*. I don't." It was actually. Her mouth was dry, her heart raced, and her knees felt oddly weak, but the barn did smell good and the rain patting on the tin roof sounded comforting.

And then he took hold of her hand again.

She wanted to pull her hand free. He'd gone too far. She wasn't the type to be so easy with a boy. Especially one she didn't know. A boy with a reputation. She had her good name to think of, her family's. "Let me go, Eli."

He released her immediately. "You haven't asked me about the burns on my hands, the injuries I got by coming to your rescue and saving you from a fiery death." He held out his hands. They were lean hands, a working man's hands.

"See that? And that?" He indicated two tiny blisters and a faint redness. "I may need to see an English doctor—go to the hospital."

Ruth could hardly hold back a giggle. "That? That's the smallest blister I've ever seen, Eli. You boys in Belleville must be sissies, to make such a fuss about a little burn like that."

"Say it again." He stared intently at her, making her warm all over again.

"What?"

"Eli. Say my name again. I like the way you say it."

Ruth clutched the quilt bag to her chest. "I have to go. I—"

"Ruth?" Irwin pulled open the heavy Dutch door of the barn. "Teacher wants to know what's taking so long."

"Coming." Quickly, she scrambled down, ignoring the offer of assistance from Eli's outstretched hand.

He chuckled and put a finger to his lips. "I won't say a word," he promised. "What happened here in the barn will be our secret."

"We have no secrets," she said and marched stiffly away, trying to salvage some shred of dignity.

If Irwin knew that she hadn't been alone in the buggy, he made no mention of it. She went back to the house. As she neared the sitting-room entrance, she heard Aunt Martha's raised voice.

"She's not getting any younger, Hannah. What was

wrong with Bennie Mast, I ask you? Eats a little too hearty, maybe, but a good boy, from a good family. I'm telling you, she's too choosy, your Ruth."

"She's that," Aunt Alma joined in. "And I heard she turned down Alf King, wouldn't even ride home from the singing with him. If she's not careful, she'll miss out on the best catches. She'll end up marrying some Ohio widower twice her age."

Ruth stopped short. Bad enough she'd made a fool of herself in the barn, but now her aunt was holding her up as an old maid, someone who couldn't get a husband. She couldn't believe they were talking about this again. Why wouldn't they understand that she couldn't accept Bennie or Alf or the other boys who'd wanted to drive her home from a young people's singing? Why couldn't she make them see that her duty was to remain at home to take care of Susanna and her mother? That not every woman could or even should have a husband and children of her own? Mam needed her. Her little sister needed her. Her responsibility was to her family.

"Here's your bag, Mam," she said too loudly as she entered the room. "So many buggies in the yard, it took a while to find ours." That wasn't dishonest, was it? Or had her foolishness with Eli Lapp caused her to make up lies as well?

"Look at these colors," Mam said as she took the bag from Ruth. "Barely faded in all these years. And such beautiful needlework. I vow, Johanna, you must have inherited your great-great-grandmother's gift with stitchery."

Ruth settled gratefully into her empty seat and picked up her square of cloth. She would make up for her wasted time in the barn, and she would forget Eli and his inappropriate behavior. It would have been a much easier task if the memory of his hand on hers wasn't so real or if she could forget how nice it had been sitting next to him in the privacy of the big barn. No boy had ever made her feel that way before.

Hazel Zook's round cheeks and pink laughing mouth rose to haunt Eli, replacing the image of Ruth Yoder's angelic face in his mind. He picked up his pace as he strode back across the wet fields toward his uncle's house. Glimpses of that night flashed in his head. He'd put miles and months between him and Hazel, but it wasn't enough. He just couldn't get her and what had happened off his conscience.

Light rain hit him in the face as he walked, and he wondered if coming to Seven Poplars might have been a mistake. Maybe he should have run farther, gone into the English world and never looked back. He wondered what was keeping him from taking that final step? He was already lost to his own faith. People would never let him forget what had happened back in Belleville.

What was he thinking coming here? Was he going to ruin another woman's life now? Ruth Yoder was a nice girl, a girl from a strict family and church. She deserved respect. And the best thing he could do for her was to stay away. He should never have gone to the Beachys' tonight.

Better choices.

He wished things could have been different, that he'd made a better choice that night at the bonfire. He wished he'd done the right thing, but now it was too late. There was no going back and no changing what had happened.

The bishops and the preachers said that God was merciful; they preached it every service. They said you could be forgiven any sin if you truly repented, and maybe that was true. But what they didn't say was how you could forgive yourself.

Chapter Five

The following Monday afternoon, Ruth left Susanna and Anna baking bread to walk to the school. Mam wanted to work on lesson plans after supper, and Ruth had offered to carry her heavy books home for her. It was so rare that Ruth had time alone to think, and it was such a pretty day that she enjoyed having the errand.

Eli Lapp and how to handle him was foremost in her mind. It was clear that he wasn't going to stop following her around until she made him understand that he was wasting his time with her. She needed to explain that it was nothing against him; she had no plans to marry anyone.

Still, she had to admit that she liked being told she was pretty, and that he was both clever and attractive. Vanity, she feared, was one of her sins. After all the talk about her being an old maid, it was nice that someone liked her, but it had to stop. The trouble was, she didn't know what she should say to Eli. How could she tell him to quit courting her when he'd said nothing about wanting her for his girlfriend? What if he laughed at her? What if he told her that she had completely misunderstood, and she was the last girl he would consider as a wife?

And then there was the problem of Irwin. The boy had

promised Mam that he'd meet her at the schoolhouse on Saturday, but he hadn't shown up, and she'd had no opportunity to speak to him alone at church. Ruth wondered if Irwin had come to school today and if Mam had been able to question him about the fire.

Eli Lapp hadn't attended the Sunday services, but that hadn't kept him from being the center of attention. Hearing the girls giggling about how handsome he was, or the mothers repeating that Eli was just the sort of boy that Preacher Reuben warned them about, was no help.

"Shepherds of our church must be diligent to protect our lambs," Aunt Martha had warned a group of mothers. "The loose ways of the world threaten our faith."

Ruth wondered if her father would have agreed with Aunt Martha, or would he have made Eli welcome and tried to turn him back to the Plain ways? Ruth hadn't done anything wrong in the barn, but if people knew she'd been alone in the buggy in the barn with Eli, her reputation could be tarnished. For all she knew, Irwin was the kind of person to tell tales, and that worried her. It wasn't necessary to simply avoid wrongdoing, but a Plain person had to avoid the perception of wrongdoing as well.

For an instant, just as Ruth rounded the bend through the trees, she remembered the schoolhouse as she'd seen it the day of the fire, and a knot rose in her throat. So many bad things could have happened. But this time, there was no smoke or the scent of smoke. School was out for the afternoon, but a few of the boys had remained for a game of softball on the grassy field. Samuel Mast's buggy was there, as well as Roman's big team and wagon, the horses standing nose to nose at the hitching rail.

When Ruth entered the schoolroom by the temporary steps, she found Roman, Samuel and her mother deep in conversation about the building repairs. Mam was smiling, and it sounded as though she was getting her wish for more room. The hand-drawn plans spread out on the desk enlarged the main area by the size of the original cloakroom and included a new porch with an inside sink and water faucet.

"Isn't this wonderful?" Mam exclaimed. "We'll be able to add eight more desks and a new cloakroom."

"Will it be done in time for the new school year?" Ruth asked, looking over the drawing.

Roman nodded. "With Eli to help, we'll finish by September."

"So Eli's good with his hands," Samuel observed.

"*Ya*, he's a fine craftsman, that boy."

"You can go on home," Mam urged, resting her hand on Ruth's arm. "We've still got things to discuss here, but there's no need for you to wait for me. If you can take the reading books and the big arithmetic book, I can manage the rest."

Ruth gathered up all the texts, including the oversize cursive writing book, said goodbye, and walked out of the school. She had just started toward the woods when Eli stepped out from behind the shed.

"Don't pop out at people like that," she said. Her cheeks felt as warm as if she'd been standing over a kettle of simmering jam. Just being near him scrambled her wits and made her tongue thick, and she was immediately more annoyed with herself than with him. She was a woman grown and should have more sense.

Worse still, Ruth had the sinking feeling that Eli knew the effect he had on her. "What do you want?" she asked.

"Does a person have to want something or can a person just say hello?"

He had a good point, but she certainly wasn't going to tell him that.

"Where are you going?" he asked.

She moved around him and continued walking. "Home."

In two strides, he caught up with her and scooped the books out of her arms. "These are heavy. Let me drive you in Uncle Roman's wagon."

"I prefer to walk." She tried to retrieve Mam's textbooks, but Eli held fast to them.

"I guess you can take them in the wagon if you want to." Ruth walked away. "Just leave them on our porch."

"I'll walk." He chuckled as he caught up. "You're stubborn, aren't you, Ruth Yoder? Miriam said you were."

All the Yoder girls were a handful. He liked that, and he liked their mother, Hannah. It wasn't often you found a widow teaching school. He thought the whole family was a breath of fresh air, even if Ruth could be as prickly as a green briar vine. He'd never known a girl to be so immune to his charms.

"When did you talk to Miriam? Certainly not at church."

"I'm not much for church. Not lately."

He had stayed away from church services yesterday because he had wanted to make sure he didn't see her. No, that wasn't true. He probably would have stayed away just the same. He didn't feel at ease at a worship service anymore. He couldn't see where he would ever be the type of man God would want. He had considered going, had gone so far as to ask Aunt Fannie to iron his good shirt and trousers, but in the end, he'd just stuffed them back in the drawer and gone off to the Dover Mall on his scooter. Instead of worship, he'd spent his afternoon feeding tokens into a video game box. His father would have been proud of him...a chip off the old ice block.

"I heard you were *rumspringa*. I suppose you like English ways."

"Some. Maybe."

"I suppose you drink beer," she accused.

"*Ne.* I don't drink alcohol. I never have." He never understood why anyone would want to drink a substance that made them angry or foolish or made them act as they never would have sober. He looked into Ruth's warm brown eyes, and for just a second, he saw a flash of compassion.

"I didn't mean to accuse you," she said in a gentler voice. "It's just that I know it goes on. I hear lots of *rumspringa* boys do."

"Girls, too," he admitted. "But not me. When I was eight, my older brother was riding in a car with some guys who were drinking. He was killed in an accident. I never thought it was something I wanted to do." He swallowed hard. Why had he told her that? He rarely felt comfortable sharing his feelings. It wasn't something a man did...not something he did.

She stopped and faced him. "I'm sorry. I didn't know." Her tone was suddenly tender, her voice sweet.

He nodded, too full of emotion to answer for a long moment, then he said, "Free, my brother, was funny, and he used to take me fishing sometimes."

"It's hard to lose someone you love." She started toward home again. "My dat died two years ago. I miss him every day."

Somehow Eli sensed that everything had changed between them. He was walking beside her, and they weren't arguing. They were just talking like friends, talking as though he'd known her his whole life.

"My dat died, too, when I was young. I don't remember

much about him, just him laughing and me jumping out of the hayloft into his arms." He hesitated. "Mam never talked about him much."

"Did your mother remarry? My aunts are urging Mam to, but I don't think she's ready."

"My stepfather, Joseph, is my father's second cousin. He married my mother when I was four, but I never thought of him as a father, just Joseph. He already had his own sons. He never liked Free and me much, and he was strict."

Ruth reached down to pluck a wild daisy from an open space beside the path. She brushed the flower petals over her lips and asked, "Is your mother happy with him? Is he a good man?"

"Joseph is a hard worker. He provides for her." He shrugged. "I never asked Mam if she was happy. In my family, you don't talk about private things."

She nodded. "My dat was different than a lot of men I know. He laughed when he was happy, shouted when he was mad and wasn't ashamed to shed a tear when our old collie died. He used to talk to us about everything."

"He must have been a special man. I wish I could have known him," Eli said. Uncle Roman was the closest he'd ever had to a father figure, and because of the distance, he hadn't seen too much of him until he'd been invited to live with them and work at the shop. "I think my uncle Roman is a little like that," he admitted. "It seems like he's a man who talks."

"*Ya,* we all love Roman." She smiled at him with her eyes. "Roman says you're talented with your hands. Your stepfather must have taught you woodworking—"

"*Ne.* My grandfather taught me his trade. I was apprenticed to him after my brother died. Mam had a new baby and I went to live with my grandparents. It was better for Mam that way." He paused for a second. "Enough talk about me." Eli's mood changed swiftly. Their conversation was becoming too intimate, and he wasn't comfortable. He forced a grin. "Why doesn't a girl your age have a steady beau?"

"That's a rude question."

"I just wondered. I mean, you're pretty, smart, and I hear you aren't afraid to make a sharp deal with the English tourists at Spence's."

"Miriam talks too much."

He laughed. "She does talk a lot." Not three days ago, he'd promised himself he wouldn't have anything more to do with Ruth Yoder. And here he was, walking her home with an armload of schoolbooks like some grass-green boy too baby-faced to shave. And saying things he'd never said to another girl.

What had made him tell Ruth about Free? He should have gotten over Free's death a long time ago. Hadn't his grandfather insisted he had gone to a better place, and only a selfish boy would want him back? But that was hard to accept then and still was now. Somehow, he felt he would never get over losing his brother, and that everything had started to go wrong, not when Dat had walked out, but the night Free had gone out joy-riding and never come back.

When they reached the stile at the fence line, Eli dared Ruth to jump and offered to catch her. He didn't mean any harm, but he would have liked to have circled her small waist with his hands and to get close enough to smell the sweet shampoo she used on her hair.

But Ruth was having none of it. She scrambled down the steps and hurried on ahead of him. As they crossed the fence, the closeness between them seemed to evaporate. Now she was just an attractive girl, and he was just a stranger with a bad reputation.

"Oh, no!" Ruth cried. "The cows are out."

Eli looked in the direction she was pointing. A heifer was trotting down the rows of ankle-high corn, snatching mouthfuls of newly sprouted field corn and munching for all she was worth. Ruth snatched off her apron and, waving it, ran toward the wayward animal.

"Shoo! Bossy! Get back!"

Eli placed the stack of books on a dry tuft of grass and dashed after her. Another cow, a black and white one wearing a bell around her neck, was just loping into the cornfield. And behind her, on a plow horse, came Ruth's sister Miriam, riding astride, skirts up around her knees and *Kapp* flying off her head. A Shetland sheepdog ran after them barking.

Since Ruth seemed to have the heifer on the run, Eli turned to cut off another cow. Yet another cow, followed by a calf, appeared on the far side of the field. Eli waved to Miriam and pointed. "I'll get this one!" he shouted. Miriam dug her bare heels into the horse's sides and lumbered after the runaway mother and baby through the corn.

The three of them had rounded up the escapees and were just driving the four animals into the barnyard when Samuel Mast's buggy came up the lane.

"Oh, no," Ruth groaned. She dropped the broken cornstalk she'd been using as a switch and hastily tied on her apron and tucked the worst of the loose strands of flyaway hair under her *Kapp.* "It's Samuel and my mother. We're in trouble now."

Miriam slid down off the horse and shook her lavender skirt over her ankles. "You'd better get away while you can," she whispered to Eli.

Eli glanced from one sister to the other. "Me? What did I do? You were the one on the horse." He pointed to Miriam, then hooked a thumb in Ruth's direction. "And Ruth just helped to catch—"

Miriam wrinkled her nose and tsk-tsked. "I'm telling you, you should go. Hannah Yoder doesn't lose her temper often, but when she does, no one is spared."

Hannah was climbing unaided out of the buggy. She looked at the cows, then back at the three of them, took a book from Samuel and started toward them. Samuel frowned, clicked to his mare and sent her trotting back down the lane in less time than it took Ruth to close the pound gate.

"What is this?" Hannah demanded.

"The cows were in the corn," Eli began. "We were just—"

"Thank you for your help. Come again another day, Eli Lapp," she said, her tone clipped. "I wish to speak to my daughters about their behavior. And it is best if you leave us in private."

He hesitated. "I left your books back in the field. I'll just—"

"Ruth will fetch the books." Hannah's eyes flashed. "You will come for dinner on Sunday. It is not a church Sunday, and I've already invited your uncle Roman and aunt Fannie. Now, you can help best by leaving us."

Eli felt his face flush. "They did nothing wrong."

"It is not your place to decide," Hannah retorted. "Your uncle was looking for you. Best you hurry back to the school. Now."

Eli looked at Ruth, excited at the thought of having Sunday dinner with her, feeling guilty about abandoning her, but Hannah was obviously giving him no choice in either matter. "Sunday, then," he said. "I'll be here Sunday for dinner." Abruptly, he turned on his heel and strode back toward the cornfield and the path that led to the school. Ruth's mother might have the reputation of being a pleasant woman, but now...

Now, he wouldn't want to be on the receiving end of whatever she would have to say to her daughters.

"Mam," Ruth started, as soon as Eli was out of earshot. "It's not Miriam's fault. She was alone here when the cows got loose."

"Not exactly alone," Miriam admitted. "Anna and Susanna are in the house, and Irwin was here."

"Irwin?" Mam demanded. "Irwin? What was he doing here?"

"He came to talk to you. He thought you'd be home from school. He was helping me move the cows from the little pasture into the pound next to the barn, and…" She left her sentence unfinished.

"Where's the boy now?" Mam rested both hands on her hips.

"I told him to go home," Miriam answered.

"Mam, it was an accident that they got out," Ruth said quickly. "She just thought she could get them in quick if she took the horse."

"To have Samuel and that boy see my daughter riding astride a horse, bareback, no shoes, no stockings, like some…some English jockey?"

Mam didn't get loud when she was angry, but her words cut like briars.

"I'm sorry, Mam," Miriam said. "I won't do it again."

"Is this the first time you've ridden the horses?"

Miriam sighed.

"Or the second?"

"Ne."

Ruth reached for her sister's hand. "Mam…don't be angry."

"You be quiet," Mam said. "I'm not speaking to you. I'm speaking to your sister." She folded her arms over her chest. "Isn't it bad enough that I had to listen to your aunt

Martha chastise me in front of everyone at the quilting because you rode on Eli Lapp's motorcycle?"

"Mam, that's not fair," Miriam protested. "It was just a ride and an ice-cream cone. And he bought one for Susanna, too. He's nice, Mam. He didn't mean any harm."

"I'm at my wits' end with you, Miriam. You are not a boy. You are a girl, a Plain girl."

Miriam burst into tears and ran toward the house.

"Miriam," Ruth called after her.

"You're almost as much to blame as she is," Mam said, turning on Ruth. "When you saw her on that horse, you should have told her to get down, not encouraged her."

"I'm sorry, Mam." Ruth met her mother's gaze. "You're right. I should have told her to get down the minute I saw her."

Mam sighed, her face softening. "It's only that I want my girls to be good women. Good Plain women."

"I think we are, most of the time," Ruth dared.

To Ruth's surprise Mam smiled faintly. "I think you are, too. Now, come." She headed toward the house. "There are chores to be done and Miriam's dander to be smoothed."

Ruth nodded. She could understand Mam's concern for Miriam's behavior, but she knew her sister, too. Miriam didn't mean to break the rules about riding horses, showing her legs and losing her *Kapp*. She was just high-spirited. Inside, where it mattered most, Miriam's soul was pure and truly Plain.

Hurrying to catch up with Mam, Ruth took hold of her hand. "Please don't be upset with yourself. You were right and we were wrong. You're the best mother in the world," she said and meant every word. "Dat would be so proud of you."

"I hope so," Mam replied. "I worry about raising you girls…if I'm doing right."

"You are," Ruth assured her, but a small shiver of unease made goose bumps raise on her arms. Mam was the wisest woman she knew. If Mam didn't always know the best thing to do, how could she ever hope to make the right choices?

Chapter Six

"I'm not going," Ruth said. "Anna and Miriam and Susanna can go without me." She turned the handle on the butter churn as hard as she could. Already specks of yellow were showing in the thick, rich cream.

"Are your arms tired? I'll help," Anna offered. It was a rainy afternoon, and they were all gathered in the kitchen. Anna was pressing the wrinkles out of her starched *Kapp* as Susanna eagerly slathered generous gobs of marshmallow filling on her still-warm chocolate cookies and pressed them together, forming fat whoopie pies. Miriam's sleeves were rolled up as she scoured the stovetop vigorously, while their mother sat at the table shelling peas.

"You should all go," Mam advised. "Young people should be together and have fun."

Ruth turned the crank harder. The butter was forming into chunks now. If there was one thing she could do, it was make beautiful, sweet butter. She loved the process, feeling the soft, squishy butter in her hands, adding just the right amount of salt and waiting to see if the blocks came out of Mam's wheat-patterned mold in perfect shapes. Not everyone could make good butter. It was the only chore in the kitchen where she could outdo Anna, and she took secret satisfaction in her gift. "I'm getting too old for singings," she said, giving the handle another turn. "It's for the younger girls and boys."

"Nonsense," Mam declared. "Samuel told me that tonight there will be wagons to take you to the homes where there are shut-ins. Your hymns will give them so much pleasure, and you know that God has given you a rare voice."

Ruth unscrewed the lid on the churn and dumped the ball of butter into a clean cloth. "Making butter is messy," she said, trying to change the subject. She did love to sing. Secretly, she wanted to go with the young people, but she was afraid. What if Eli was there? What would she say to him? What would he say to her? She sighed. She was probably making something out of nothing. If Eli was there, he probably wouldn't even notice her with all the other girls there.

"Like life," Mam said.

"What?" Ruth asked.

Mam motioned with her chin. "You said making butter is messy, and I said, 'It's like life.'" She chuckled. "But when everything goes right, you are left with a treasure."

"I wasn't even sure you would let us go to the singing," Ruth said.

"Aren't you afraid we'll do something scandalous again?" Miriam chimed in.

Their mother fixed the two of them with a cool gaze. "I was upset," Mam admitted. "And let my temper get the best of me. I know you are both good girls. It's just that you have a reckless nature, Miriam." Her stern look melted to a smile. "You're too much like me, I fear."

"Like you?" Susanna licked a sticky finger. "You would never ride a horse like a boy and show your legs."

Mam tossed a pea shell at her. "Not only would," she admitted. "Did."

"Mam!" Anna said in astonishment.

Ruth's eyes widened in surprise. "You didn't! Did you?" It was hard to imagine her mother breaking the rules.

"Not even Mennonite girls were allowed to enter the horse race for the Amish boys at the Harrington fair when I was young." Mischief sparked in Mam's eyes. "So I borrowed my cousin's clothing, pinned my braids up under his straw hat, and used his name to enter the race."

"You rode in a boys' race?" Susanna demanded. *"Ne!"*

"I tried. I got as far as the first turn on the track before my hat blew off and my hair tumbled down. Everyone laughed."

"But you won the race, didn't you, Mam?" Ruth said. She was laughing now with the others.

"Tell us," Miriam urged. "You did."

Mam grimaced. "I did not. The boys were so surprised that half of them reined in their horses, and two of the riders crashed into each other. My pony reared up, and I fell off, right in front of the grandstand." She shook her head. "It was years before people stopped teasing me about it."

Susanna's eyes widened in excitement. "Were you in trouble?"

"Big trouble." Mam covered her face with her hands, remembering. She dropped them. "You see, at the time, I was thinking about what I wanted to do instead of what was best for my family or our community. People blamed my parents because I broke the rules."

"It was a bad rule," Miriam said. "Girls should be able to ride in races."

"Maybe," Mam agreed, "but rules are made for a reason. If they are unfair, people should work together to change them. But no one, least of all a silly thirteen-year-old girl, should decide what rules she will follow and what she will ignore. Because I broke the rule, riders or their mounts could have been badly hurt."

"I understand," Ruth said. Then she giggled. "But I would have liked to have seen you dressed up like a boy."

"It probably wasn't as good a disguise as I thought," their mother admitted.

"So Miriam takes after you," Ruth said thoughtfully as she began to squeeze the liquid out of the yellow butter. "And look how well you turned out."

Her mother shook her head. "I work hard every day to be the type of woman I believe God and my community expect. We all have parts of our nature that need constant care, lest, like an unweeded garden, the unpleasant things spring up and choke out the good."

Susanna stuck the last pair of cakes together. "Weeds, Mam? How could you grow weeds?"

"I could," Mam teased. "Right out of my hair, so that I couldn't get my *Kapp* on."

Susanna laughed and they all laughed with her. Then she glanced at Ruth. "I want to ride in the wagon and sing songs. Will you come, Roofie? Please."

Ruth pressed the new butter tightly into the mold. "We'll see," she said. "We'll see." But she knew she would. She knew that she couldn't bear to stay away and miss the evening of fun…and just maybe the chance to see Eli again.

Eli unbuttoned the top button on his good shirt because he felt like his collar was choking him and drained the last of the root beer in his paper cup. Lots of young people from three churches had arrived at the Borntragers' barn for the singing, and the straw wagons were already filling up with chattering girls in starched *Kapps* and aprons. The boys and young men hung back, some playing a loud game of dodgeball, but most just watching to see which girls would climb into which wagon. Every boy wanted to choose his wagon wisely, depending on which girl he was sweet on, and no one wanted to appear too eager to climb on amid all those blue, purple and green dresses.

Eli hadn't wanted to come. What if Ruth Yoder was here? He'd made up his mind that being around her was a mistake. He kept telling himself that the only reason he felt such a strong attraction to her was that he was a long way from home and all his friends. He might have a bad reputation in Belleville, but at least everyone knew him. There, he felt a part of the community. Here, he just stood out.

Maybe he should do what everyone had expected when he left home, leave and turn Mennonite or even English. He had a trade. He could get work, get a driver's license and buy a car. Other boys and even a few girls he knew had done it. Then he wouldn't have to live by the strict rules of being Amish. He could do anything he wanted.

So why was he here? He'd promised himself when he left his grandfather's house that he would choose his own path. He'd spent half his life in a household where religion dictated every hour of the day. He'd never been whipped, never gone without food or a clean bed, but his grandparents had seen him as a way to make up for his father's mistakes. They were determined that he would live a moral life, that he not leave the church. Sadly, their attitude had done more to turn him against the Amish lifestyle than they could ever imagine. In their quest to save him, his grandparents had dedicated their lives to raising him in a somber house without laughter, where charity was freely given to others, but withheld from their own grandson.

That wasn't to say life in Belleville had been bad. Some

things about his growing up had been good. He'd loved the old farm and the stillness of his grandfather's orderly wood-shop, the clean scent of the shavings that fell from the lathe, the feel of cherry or walnut or pine taking shape under his fingers. He'd taken pleasure in the carefully cared-for tools and the furniture and cabinets that the shop produced. And he'd found sinful pride in his gift for making a chest of drawers or a table that would last for centuries and only become more beautiful with the years.

Sometimes in the long hours he spent alone in the shop, he had imagined Jesus as a humble carpenter in his own shop. If he had lived in those old times, Eli wondered if he and the Lord might have been able to talk about a par-ticular slab of wood or the patience it took to achieve a hand-rubbed shine on a tabletop. And he wondered if the Lord could have explained why Eli's brother had had to die in a ditch before his life had really begun.

Eli glanced around, feeling more out of place by the second. He shouldn't have come here tonight. He'd only done it to please Aunt Fannie and because he liked to sing. He had a good voice and a good memory for the old hymns in High German. Singing at service and young people's gatherings had always been one outlet that hadn't displeased his grandparents.

"Go," Aunt Fannie had urged him. "Meet the young people. You'll make friends. Go to the singing."

Uncle Roman had shrugged. "Go and take the small buggy," he'd offered. "Maybe you'll find a girl who'll let you drive her home."

Small chance of that. But just in case, he'd curried Uncle Roman's bay gelding until his hide gleamed and polished his hooves with lamp black. He'd washed down the buggy and shined the wheels. And he'd replaced some of the ordi-nary lights required by law on the back of the buggy with flashing blue bulbs. There wasn't any sense in having the reputation of being wild if you didn't make the most of it.

Singings were supposed to be fun, to be a healthy way for young people to get to know each other, for forming friendships that led to marriage. Tonight's procession would go from house to house. They would remain long enough to sing a selection of hymns and then pile back onto the wagons to go to the next house. And the rule was, everyone had to switch wagons at each stop. The scramble to get together with the boy or girl you liked, without the adult chaperones catching on, was tricky.

A young man, Mahlon something—Eli didn't know his last name—was the singing leader for the evening. Mahlon shouted out for everyone to climb on the wagons, that it was time to leave. If Eli wasn't going to go, this was his opportunity to slip away without anyone noticing. He'd spoken to a few guys he'd met already, tossed a few balls, had a soda and a doughnut, but no one would notice if he didn't go with the group. He could drive around for an hour or two in his uncle's buggy, and then go home. Aunt Fannie would never know the difference.

Eli was just sidling toward his horse and buggy when he heard a high squeal and spotted Miriam in the lead wagon, tugging on a younger girl's hand. On the ground, giving the plump girl in the blue dress a push up, stood Ruth. Tonight she was in purple. Her *Kapp* was neatly in place, hiding every strand of red hair; her stockings were pressed smooth, her apron was blindingly white and her shoes were shined. The face under the white *Kapp* was so full of life, so beautiful, it made his breath catch in his throat.

A boy took Ruth's hand and helped her up, and the driver clicked to the team. The big Percheron draft horses broke into a trot, and the second team pranced and strained at the reins, eager to follow. Other boys hurried to catch up and leaped on the wagon of their choice, some making quite a show of it.

Eli stood watching. He could just see the back of Ruth's *Kapp* as her wagon rolled away. At the last possible minute, Eli made up his mind. He dashed after the third wagon and hopped on beside a skinny teen in a green dress and black sneakers. She flashed a big smile at him and slid over to make room, patting the seat beside her. Eli gave her a hesitant smile and wondered if this was going to be a long evening.

Ruth was glad she'd given in and come when she saw the smile on old Warren Troyer's face. Warren's mother was ninety and in a wheelchair. She was so crippled up in her body that she seemed no bigger than an eight-year-old child. Her pinched face was as lined as a dried apple, but her eyes gleamed with pleasure, and she clapped her small wrinkled hands with joy. Susanna wiggled with excitement as Mahlon led the group into another song. Willard and Amy had set up a long table with sandwiches, chips, cookies and jugs of apple juice.

Ruth was so glad Mam had urged her to come. Riding the wagons, singing the old songs was as much fun as it had always been. And she had to admit that Mahlon's attention wasn't unwelcome. Even if she didn't want a beau, it was nice that she had someone to talk to besides her girlfriends and sisters.

At each house, the groups had formed into two sections, one of boys and one of girls. Both sounded good tonight, all the male and female voices blending in. A deep, rich male voice behind her made Ruth glance over her shoulder. To her surprise, she saw Eli Lapp standing beside Mahlon.

She hadn't expected that Eli, of all people, would know the words to the hymns or would have such a gift for singing. Miriam noticed him, too. Ruth saw her sister smile at him. She would have to make certain that Miriam remained with her when they got back on the wagons and that they picked one that Eli wasn't riding on. Mam had just gotten herself calmed down. It would not do to give Aunt Martha something more to gossip about.

Later, at the refreshment table, Ruth was telling Amy Troyer how good her ham sandwiches were when someone thrust a cup of juice into her hand. When she turned to say thank you, Eli Lapp was grinning down at her. Standing this close to him, she realized just how tall he was. Her fingers closed around the cup.

"Nothing special," Amy said. "Boiled ham and home-made mustard. I can give you the recipe for the mustard if you like."

"Ya," Ruth answered. "Mam would like it."

"Everything is good," Eli agreed. There were lots of pretty girls here tonight, but none of them shone as brightly as Ruth Yoder. He hadn't guessed that she had such a beautiful voice, so sweet that it gave him shivers down his spine.

Mahlon shouted for the young people to gather for a prayer before they got back on the wagons. Ruth and Eli moved off with the others to the porch where the bishop waited. "What wagon are you getting on?" Eli whispered.

The bishop was beginning to offer the prayer.

"Shh," Ruth whispered. She closed her eyes, all too conscious of Eli standing very close on one side of her and Mahlon on the other.

"Have a safe night," the bishop said when he had finished. "Be careful and enjoy yourselves."

Eli leaned down. "Ride with me, Ruth," he said, trying to keep the eagerness out of his voice.

"It's best if I don't. We wouldn't want anyone to get the wrong idea."

Eli stiffened.

Ruth heard Mahlon chuckle.

"She's riding home in my buggy tonight," Mahlon said.

Eli looked into Ruth's eyes, and in the illumination of the carriage lamp, for just a second, she caught a flash of deep disappointment.

And then he turned, uttered a sound of wry amusement and walked away, trying to tell himself that it didn't mean a thing, trying to convince himself that one pretty girl was like another, when all the while he knew better.

"I did not say *'ya'* to riding home with you, Mahlon," Ruth said. "That was an untruth. I have my own buggy, and I have every intention of driving Susanna home in it."

She should have been pleased by Mahlon's attention, but she felt bad for Eli. It had to be hard to come to a new place with new faces. Mahlon could have been nicer to him, at least invited him to join them in the wagon for the next leg of the trip. Mahlon knew very well that he and she were just friends, and he knew her well enough that he understood that she wasn't looking for a husband. "Why don't you take Anna?" she suggested. "She likes you."

"And I like Anna," he said. "I just like you better."

"I haven't changed my mind," she pointed out, looking for Eli in the sea of boys in colored shirts. Blue. His had been blue...the color of his eyes. She didn't see him anywhere.

"Come on, let me drive you home. Anna and Miriam can take your little sister home safely enough." Mahlon took her hand and pulled her back to the first wagon. "On to the Millers' place," he told the driver, then looked back. "Have we got everyone?"

Ruth glanced around, saw Susanna and Anna in the second wagon and settled back into the straw. The evening had started out so well, but now she was feeling out of sorts. She wished she could just go home. As the wagon rolled down the Troyers' driveway, she looked back for Eli again, but he was still nowhere. To her surprise, she was disappointed. Disappointed she might not see those blue eyes again tonight.

It was almost ten o'clock by the time the wagons rolled down the last lane and turned back toward the Borntragers' farm. A few of the young people were still singing, but for the most part, there were more giggles and laughter than adhering to the hymns. Miriam was on the same wagon with one of her best friends, and they were teasing Harvey Borntrager, Dinah's fifteen-year-old brother-in-law. Everyone liked Harvey, but this was the first time he'd been allowed to go to a singing, and he had to expect his share of ribbing.

The evening ended on a high note with one of the other churches inviting all the young people to a day of fishing and games later in the summer. The chaperones kept close watch to see that no one was left behind as everyone found their respective buggies or, if they'd walked to the Borntragers' place, that they found their own group to go home.

Susanna had fallen asleep on the wagon, and it took both Ruth and Anna to get her down and into their buggy. Mahlon, Ruth was pleased to note, had found another girl to escort home. Ruth was just fastening the last strap on Blackie's harness when Eli appeared by the horse's head, startling her again. She met his blue-eyed gaze.

"Sure you don't want to ride with me?" he asked.

She swallowed. "I told you that I didn't think it was a good idea," she reminded him.

"Just as well," he said. He reached behind him, caught the hand of a girl standing in the shadows. "So you won't mind if I take Miriam instead?"

"I— *Ne*," she stammered. "I mean, that's not—"

"See you at home!" Miriam called excitedly, leading Eli away.

"Miriam!" Ruth tried to push Blackie's head aside so she could see her sister, but he was being stubborn. "Mam won't like it. You can't—" But once again, she was standing there helpless as her sister dashed off with Eli Lapp. She tried to convince herself as she climbed up on the bench beside the sleeping Susanna that the distress she felt was concern for Miriam, but there was no denying the truth.

Secretly, she wished she was the one sitting beside Eli on the buggy seat.

Chapter Seven

On Friday, Roman and Eli began work on the repairs at the Seven Poplars schoolhouse. Samuel had brought his farm wagon to carry away the burnt wood and pieces of foundation, and Hannah had dismissed the older boys to provide additional labor. Anna and Susanna had gone to Spence's Auction with eggs, flowers and strawberries, but Miriam had stayed behind and volunteered to carry all the school desks out into the yard and give them a good cleaning. Mam's older female students were helping. Ruth and her mother divided the remaining children into reading groups and led them away from the building to continue class outside.

Ruth found a spot under an oak tree at the edge of the school yard to spread out blankets. All her students were girls; her mother had taken the boys into the shade on the far side of the ball field. Even here, Ruth found that the loud sounds of hammering and clattering wood drew the children's attention and kept them from giving full attention to their reading lessons.

Surrendering, Ruth asked Verna Beachy to read aloud from a battered copy of *Heidi*, and that seemed to satisfy everyone. Ruth's attention, however, drifted from the story, and she glanced back at the school to see Miriam chatting with Eli as she scrubbed a desk with a wet sponge.

Ruth felt vaguely out of sorts and looked away, then back again. She hadn't spoken to Miriam about her reckless decision to ride home in the buggy with Eli after she'd already been in hot water with Mam over the motor scooter. Although everyone always knew which couples left the singing together, Amish tradition was to give young people privacy by pretending not to notice. Miriam had returned home shortly after Ruth, but Miriam hadn't dropped so much as a hint as to whether she'd enjoyed the secluded time with Eli or how he'd behaved. And Mam, who usually knew everything that went on in the household, seemed to be oblivious. It wasn't like Miriam to be so secretive, but Ruth didn't know how to ask without seeming jealous. Not that she was. Was she?

Ruth didn't know if she was more vexed with her sister or with Eli. Miriam should have better sense. What kind of boy paid attention to one sister and then the other? That wasn't the way things were done here in Kent County. And he was way too forward, to boot.

Usually a boy didn't directly ask a girl to ride home with him from a social. He'd have a friend speak to one of her friends first to see whether the girl was willing. Certainly no one ever courted two girls at the same time. That would be considered fast behavior and would invite a talking-to by Uncle Reuben or the bishop. Belleville was a long way away, but Ruth didn't think customs could be all that different in Eli's home community.

Ruth's thoughts drifted back to the other night. Had Eli been serious when he'd asked her to ride home from the singing with him? She'd refused him. So why was she feeling the green pangs of jealousy?

The unkind thought that Eli might have been using her

to get close to Miriam occurred to her. But that didn't make sense. Wasn't Miriam the one who'd first encouraged him by accepting the ride on his ridiculous motorbike at Spence's?

As far as Ruth was concerned, Eli Lapp was causing far too much trouble in Seven Poplars. The best thing Ruth and Miriam could do was stay away from him. But that was going to be hard to do now, what with him working at the school and, worse, coming to dinner.

Ruth couldn't imagine what had possessed Mam to invite him for Sunday dinner. Mam had also asked Irwin, but Mam often asked pupils to her home so that she could give them personal attention. But Eli? How were people to stop talking about Miriam riding his motorbike if Mam invited him to their house? The community would think the two were courting.

Maybe they were....

One of the first-graders climbed into Ruth's lap. Little Rosy was wide-eyed and adorable, enthralled by the tale of Heidi's adventures. Ruth couldn't help cuddling the child. As Ruth gazed around at the circle of innocent faces beneath their white caps, she was struck by the strong bonds of love that bound them all together.

Sweet or naughty, quick or slow, spirited or plodding, Ruth loved each of the girls as if they were her own sisters. It gave her a deep satisfaction to know that these young people were the future of the Amish church and community. They would guard the faith and uphold the traditions she held so dear, and most of them, God willing, would always be part of her life.

Her choice to remain unwed meant never having her own children, never sewing small *Kapps* and aprons, never watching a boy take his first steps into manhood. Ruth thought she was prepared to make that sacrifice, but this afternoon, she felt a deep sorrow at what she would be giving up. In the Amish faith, it was the hereafter that was important, not this earthly existence. But for the briefest space of time, she allowed herself to imagine her own baby in her arms, her own kitchen, and putting a hearty midday meal on the table for a husband.

Ruth's insides knotted as her overactive imagination betrayed her. In her mind, she saw a bearded man filling the kitchen doorway…a man with Eli's blue eyes, his butter-yellow hair and his roguish grin. "Something smells good, Ruth," she could almost hear him say.

"Ruth."

She blinked and focused on Verna Beachy's owl-like expression.

"The bell," Verna said.

Rosy squirmed out of Ruth's arms. "School's over," Rosy piped.

Ruth chuckled. "You're right, girls. Go on."

Laughing and chattering to each other, Elvie, Verna, Rosy and the others hurried to gather their lunch boxes and bonnets. Samuel's ten-year-old twins, Peter and Rudy, and the other younger boys were running back to the school-house as well. And almost before Ruth had folded the blankets, the children were scattering: some on push-scooters, a few on in-line skates and others running barefoot across the fields toward home.

Samuel drove the wagonload of burned wood out of the yard. There was still a great deal of hammering and crashing coming from the front of the schoolhouse, but the other men were still working. Mam had gone inside, and Ruth could see her pulling down the window shades.

Ruth started toward the building when she spied Irwin open the door to the girls' outhouse, a squirming snake clutched in his hands. He saw her and quickly tucked the snake behind his back as he let the door swing shut.

"What are you up to now?" Ruth demanded. She'd been wanting to speak to the boy ever since Miriam had told her that she was sure their cows getting out was no accident. Apparently, Miriam had gone to open the water pipes at the base of the windmill and left Irwin to fasten the gate. Miriam believed that he'd deliberately let the animals loose. "What are you doing with that snake?"

"Snake? What snake?"

Ruth saw the reptile drop and slither away. It was a black snake, at least two feet long. She stepped in front of Irwin and looked directly into his eyes. "You were trying to frighten the girls with that snake, weren't you?"

"No, I just…" He shrugged and stared at the ground.

Ruth folded her arms. "You were playing a mean trick. You know you don't belong near the girls' outhouse."

Irwin's prominent ears took on the glow of ripe tomatoes as he tried to bury his chin in his faded shirt.

She gently raised his head so that he had to meet her gaze. "You were making mischief again, weren't you? Just as you did at our house when you let the cows out."

Irwin sniffed and rubbed his nose with the back of a grubby hand.

"Don't you know that our cows could have become sick from eating the corn? Not to mention the damage to the crops. You know how valuable the animals are. Why would you do such a thing?"

He shrugged.

Ruth took a deep breath. Dealing with this child was frustrating. She forced her tone to copy her mother's, authoritarian but soft. "Mam has invited you to Sunday dinner. You *will* be there. Understand?"

Irwin nodded.

"And no more tricks. Not at the school nor at our farm. Or else."

"I won't, I promise," a man's voice said.

Ruth turned around to find a grinning Eli standing behind her. As she turned, Irwin made his escape. He dove under the fence rail and plunged down the path that led through the grove.

"You're no help," Ruth admonished Eli. She told him about the snake in the girls' outhouse.

Eli laughed. "And Irwin pleaded innocent, did he?"

"'Snake, what snake?'" She snickered. "He's impossible. You never know what he'll do next."

"Boys will be boys," he offered, palms up as if that explained it.

"Miriam thinks Irwin deliberately let our cows out. That's why she yelled at him and sent him home instead of asking him to help round them up."

Eli regarded her, his blue eyes thoughtful. "Roman thinks the kid might need more help than his cousins can give." He shook his head. "Norman and Lydia already have a full plate with their own children."

"But they're all Irwin has," Ruth said. "His parents and sister died in the fire. Where else would he go?"

"I don't know. I've been wondering the same thing." He motioned toward the school. "Wanna come inside and see what we got done today? Back at the shop, Roman and I are working on some built-in cabinets."

She looked up at him, thinking again how tall he was and how sure he sounded of himself when he talked about his skills at building. "They sound nice," she said lamely, debating whether she wanted to inspect the progress. Out here she could breathe, but for some reason, going inside with him didn't seem like all that good an idea.

Miriam came out of the school and waved. "Eli!"

Ruth took a step back, feeling as if a bubble around her and Eli had burst. It had been so nice, just talking, but the moment had passed, and she felt awkward with him again.

Glancing at Miriam, who was practically running to Eli, Ruth wondered if her sister expected her to leave the two of them alone, or should she pretend that she knew nothing about their mutual attraction?

"Mam wants us to go to the chair shop and make a phone call." Miriam reached in her pocket and pulled out a small piece of paper. "We need to make a dentist appointment for Susanna." She smiled at Eli. "Roman said you wouldn't mind driving us down in his buggy."

"Ne," Eli said. "I'll be glad to."

Miriam looked back to Ruth. "Mam wants us to call before the office closes for the afternoon."

Their church didn't allow phones in their homes, but because Roman did business with the English, the bishop had permitted him to have one installed in a small lean-to shed at the side of the chair shop. Any member of the community was free to make calls when they needed to.

Feeling like a third wheel, Ruth looked from one to the other. "No need for me to come," she offered. "I can just—"

Miriam shook her head. "Mam said *both* of us. I have the number."

"I'll go, but you're going to have to make the appointment," Ruth insisted. "You have to learn to do it sometime."

"All right," Miriam agreed. "And afterward, we can walk home."

"No trouble to drive you home," Eli insisted.

"Samuel says the board has approved our pie auction at the picnic," Miriam said as Eli went to get the buggy.

"Good." Ruth studied her sister. Miriam's cheeks were rosy and her eyes sparkling, but she hadn't so much as glanced at Eli as he walked away. Was she trying to hide her feelings for him, or was she just excited about the school frolic?

"I'm going to make a cherry pie with a lattice-top crust." Miriam chatted as they walked toward the wagon. "Have you decided what kind you'll make?"

Ruth groaned. "I don't know." She shook her head. The last time she'd attempted an apple-cranberry pie, her crust was tough and the apples in the center only half baked. "I don't really want to go. Maybe I won't even make—"

"Mam promised that we would all make one." Miriam smiled. "Even Susanna."

Ruth rolled her eyes, and they both giggled.

Eli returned with the horse and buggy and halted the animal so that they could climb in. Miriam scrambled up first, next to Eli. Luckily, the front seat was roomy enough for all three of them.

Roman's horse was a showy dapple-gray, and once they were on the road, Eli passed the leathers to Miriam. Laughing, she urged the horse into a trot. Ruth braced her feet against the boards and enjoyed the feel of the warm breeze against her face.

"Do you like music?" Eli asked.

"I do," Miriam said.

To Ruth's surprise, he reached under the seat and came up with a small boom box that played CDs. He pushed a button and Garth Brooks filled the air, singing a fast song about a rodeo rider and a thunderstorm. It was on the tip of Ruth's tongue to remind Eli that the music wasn't Plain and that Mam wouldn't approve, but she knew that Garth Brooks was one of Miriam's favorites. She had to admit that she liked country tunes herself. *Just this once,* she thought. What harm could it do?

By the time the story-song had ended and another singer, a girl, began a tune about an Appaloosa horse, the three of them were having fun laughing and tapping their feet to the music as they arrived at the chair shop all too soon. Eli clicked off the machine and tucked it back into his hiding spot as Miriam turned the gelding into the parking lot.

The main structure was about forty feet long, made of concrete block, the front faced with yellow siding. There was a big yard and storage sheds behind the chair shop. Beyond, down a short lane, stood a neat story-and-a-half house where Roman and Fannie lived with their children. Eli's aunt was in the side yard taking clothes off the line. They waved, and she waved back.

Stopping at the chair shop always made Ruth a little sad because it made her think of Dat and the times she'd come to watch him at work here when she was small. But it made her feel good, too, because rent from the building and house made it possible for Mam to provide for her family.

There were three windows along the front of the shop, all with white curtains. The Dutch door in the center was painted blue. On the wide porch two rocking chairs were displayed as examples of the furniture that Roman and Eli made.

Eli jumped out and helped Miriam down. As Ruth scooted over to climb down from the buggy, Eli looked up at her. "If you come inside, I'll show you the cabinets we're making for the school."

Ruth bit down on her lower lip, glanced at Miriam, then back at Eli again. "I should go help Miriam...in case they have any questions at the dentist's office."

"It's okay. You go," Miriam called, turning to go. "I'll be fine."

"She'll be fine," Eli repeated. His expression was bold, almost amused as he met Ruth's gaze.

"All right," Ruth said hesitantly. "I'd like to see them."

He looped the leathers over the hitching rack and returned to offer his hand as she climbed down. Tingles ran up her arm as his strong fingers closed around hers. Confused, and a little excited, Ruth's heart beat faster as she followed Eli up onto the porch and into the shop. She couldn't deny that she was attracted to him in a way that she'd never been to any other boy.

She should have turned then and gone back to the buggy, but she didn't want to. She wanted Eli to smile at her... wanted him to forget her sister and think only of her.

Roman's oldest son, Tyler, was at the corner desk in the showroom-office, poring over a math book. He grinned up at them and then sighed and applied his pencil to the yellow answer sheet with dogged determination. Eli nodded to him and led Ruth down a hall and into the workshop.

Instantly, she was enveloped in the smells of fresh sawdust, paint stripper, varnish, stain and wax. Racks of tools hung on the wall to her left, and on a wide workbench lay an unfinished, ladder-back chair. In the center of the room stood the carved headboard of an old bed in the process of painstaking restoration.

"These are for the school," Eli said, walking around the headboard to show her a length of cabinets that stood in the far corner. Ruth saw at once that these were not finished in veneer, but fashioned of thick pine boards with sturdy hinges. If there were no more fires, water or insect damage, the cabinets should serve the children well for decades.

Ruth followed him over and stroked a smooth door. "You didn't use plywood."

Eli grinned. "*Ne.* Reuben made a gift of the boards. He said they'd been drying in his grain shed for twenty years just waiting to be put to a good use. The hinges are ones we salvaged from an English job. They were just going to throw them away, so I asked if we could have them."

"Foolish, throwing them away," Ruth agreed. She fingered the nearest hinge. "But it must have been hard work to clean them."

Eli shrugged his broad shoulders. "A little elbow grease and some strong paint remover. Tyler helped."

"Mam will be so pleased." She opened a door and then closed it. "The doors fit perfectly. They don't even squeak," she teased.

"Of course they don't squeak." He laughed. "I've something else to show you. It's out back."

Ruth glanced in the direction of the front of the shop. "I should probably see how Miriam is—"

"Miriam will be fine," Eli insisted. "It's just a phone call. Come on. You'll like this even better than the schoolhouse cabinets."

Curious, Ruth followed him out of the shop across the yard and into a small shed beyond. Here, too, was a workbench and a tool chest. On the bench stood an unfinished chest with a gently rounded top. The piece was fashioned of cherry, about three feet long and no more than twenty-four inches high with bracket feet and a shiny brass lock. But it was the decoration that stunned her. Carved into the front was a strawberry plant, bursting with berries and two little birds, replicas so lifelike that she half expected them to pluck a strawberry and fly away.

"Oh," she gasped, unable to resist running her fingertips over the design. "Eli, you did this?"

His eyes lit with pleasure. "Do you like the wrens?"

She had known they were wrens. The bright eyes, the

perky tails, the boldness, they could only be Carolina Wrens. "*Ya,* I do." She hesitated. "Is this for an English customer?"

"*Ne.* For an Amish."

She nibbled at her lower lip. "It is beautiful, *ya,* but I think not Plain."

"My hands form what I see in my mind."

"But we Plain people are not of this world but the one to come."

He nodded. "If God gave me this dream, this skill, maybe He wants me to make use of it."

Ruth shivered, despite the warmth of the shed. "You must guard against the sin of pride, Eli," she chastised, unable to meet his gaze. "You are not so Plain as other men."

"As Mahlon?"

She felt her cheeks grow warm as she looked at him and then away again. The chest was the most beautiful thing she thought she had ever seen, so beautiful that it made a lump in her throat. "He is a sensible…"

Eli chuckled. "You are very serious for such a pretty girl, Ruth. You accuse me of *Hochmut,* but you seem full of pride, as well."

"Me?" Her eyes widened in surprise. This time, she didn't look away from him. "How do I show false pride?"

He shrugged. "Think about it. Doesn't it give you satisfaction that you work so hard to take care of your mother and your sisters? That you've decided to sacrifice your own life to remain on the farm and—"

"Who told you…" She swallowed in an attempt to ease the knot in her throat. She knew who'd been talking about her. Miriam. Again. "You don't understand, Eli. Someone has to—"

"I may not attend church as I should, but I spent my childhood listening to God's word. And one of the sermons I remember my grandfather giving was about martyrs. He said that only the Lord chooses martyrs. Make certain that you really know what God wants of you before you decide on a path, Ruth."

Moisture blurred her vision. Was Eli right? She backed away from him, uncertain as to what to say...to think.

"I'm sorry," he said, taking a step toward her, reaching out with one hand. "I didn't mean to—"

"Ruth!" Miriam came around the corner of the building. "There you are. I got the appointment."

Eli met Ruth's gaze again as he lowered his hand to his side. Miriam looked at one and then the other.

"Come on," Eli said, walking past Ruth and out of the shed. "Let me drive you both home."

"Ne." Ruth's voice sounded strange in her ears. "We will walk. We can cut across the pasture."

Miriam and Eli exchanged glances. Miriam chuckled. "So we walk. I'll see you on Sunday, Eli. At dinner?"

"Ya," he answered, hooking his thumbs in the waistband of his pants. "I'll be there. I wouldn't miss it."

Chapter Eight

At noon on Sunday, Ruth watched as Anna welcomed Fannie Byler into the kitchen. Dinner wasn't until one o'clock, but Fannie was Mam's dearest friend, and she'd come early to chat before the meal. Roman, Eli and the children were expected later. "Come in, come in," Anna urged, waving a wooden spoon.

Fannie's wide-brimmed black bonnet framed a plump rosy face with bright blue eyes, a snub nose and a wide smile. "I brought a lemon sponge cake," she said, after they'd all exchanged hugs.

"Wonderful," Mam said. "Anna made pies this morning. And Ruth's just finishing the coleslaw."

Anna placed Fannie's basket on the counter, and Susanna took her bonnet and cape.

"Irwin is coming," Susanna bubbled. "I think he eats a lot. He's a bad boy at school, but Mam told him he had to behave."

"Irwin's coming?" Fannie rolled her eyes.

"Mam often invites her pupils," Ruth explained, with a meaningful glance in Susanna's direction.

Mam put a finger to her lips, and Fannie nodded, catching on.

"Not likely anyone would go hungry at your table, Mam," Anna said, attempting to distract Susanna from sharing Irwin's shortcomings.

"Ne." Susanna turned to Fannie. "I carried pickled beets and applesauce up from the cellar."

Fannie fanned herself, dropped into a rocking chair and gazed with admiration at the kitchen table. Ruth poured coffee for the older women and then returned her attention to the coleslaw.

"Goodness, I'll be glad when my Clara and Alice are a little older," Fannie said, not in the least put out that Mam had cut off her question about Irwin. "These girls of yours are a marvel." She poured a dollop of thick cream into her coffee and stirred in three spoons of honey.

It was always nice to have Fannie and her family at the dinner table. If Ruth could only be as pleased with their other dinner guests. She knew it wasn't her place to question who her mother invited to Sunday dinner, but she didn't trust Irwin, and Eli...

She didn't know where in her head to begin with Eli or what to do with all the emotions he stirred up. He troubled her, with those rumors of his reputation. He just looked like trouble. And gossip or not, there had to be some truth to what Alma had said about him, didn't there? Alma wouldn't just make up such a terrible story, not even about a stranger. And it wasn't just the gossip that made Ruth uncomfortable. There was something more about Eli. It was the way he had made her uncertain about the life decisions she'd made. And then there was the matter of Miriam. She couldn't deny that Eli was exciting, but at the same time, she was afraid that her sister was becoming too attached to him.

Abruptly, she yawned and covered her mouth with the back of her hand. Thinking about that beautiful chest with the carved birds and the fear that Eli had made it for

Miriam had kept her awake until after midnight last night. By the light of day, Ruth knew the idea was preposterous, but silly notions did that to you at night sometimes; they made you totally illogical.

"Roofie?" Susanna was standing beside her, a sugar bowl in her hand. "Can I put the sugar in now?"

"Just a minute." Ruth began to stir mayonnaise and lemon juice into the grated slaw. "Now," she said to Susanna.

Susanna carefully carried the sugar bowl back to the table. Watching her, Ruth couldn't help but smile. Susanna was such a sweet soul. Dat had been right. She was a blessing to their family. Eli didn't understand why Ruth had made the decisions she had. God had trusted her family with Susanna, and it was only right that Ruth be here to care for her. It was selfish to consider anything else. Some day, Mam would grow old, and they both would need strong hands to support them.

"It was good of you to ask Eli to dinner," Fannie was saying to Mam. "He's a good boy, no matter what some people say. I'm hoping that if families like yours welcome him, others will."

Mam glanced at Anna. "Could you help Susanna find a clean *Kapp* and apron?"

Since it was just the family this morning, her sisters had covered their freshly washed hair with kerchiefs, but would need *Kapps* before male company arrived. "I can do it," Ruth offered. "I'm ready, and I finished the slaw."

"*Ne.*" Anna caught Susanna's hand. "Come on, Susanna-banana. I'll braid your hair." Susanna giggled and followed her out of the kitchen.

When Susanna was safely out of earshot, Fannie spoke softly. "I know you've both heard the rumors about Eli, but I wanted you to know I don't believe them. There are things the boy isn't telling us. Roman says he has a good heart."

Ruth tried not to listen, but it was impossible not to hear Mam's reply. "I keep telling Martha and Alma it's wrong to judge Eli without proof."

Fannie sniffed. "That Alma asked me straight out if Eli was shunned in Belleville. He wasn't." She leaned close to Mam and lowered her voice. "Roman thinks the world of his sister Esther, but he thinks she's ill-treated Eli. You know about Eli's real father, don't you?"

Mam shook her head.

"He left the Old Order Amish church. Went to the English." Fannie glanced across the kitchen. Ruth concentrated on prying open a plastic container of sesame seeds.

"You needn't fear to speak in front of Ruth," Mam soothed. "She'd not spread ill about anyone." She chuckled. "Our Susanna is another story. She means no harm, but whatever she hears…"

"Well, it's no secret," Fannie continued. "The way Roman tells it, Eli's father abandoned his family and his faith. He always had an eye for worldly ways. He liked the English women with their legs all bare and their bosoms showing, and they liked him, too. One day, when he was plowing, he just left his team in the field and walked away."

Ruth couldn't contain her curiosity. "He just abandoned his family?"

Fannie nodded. "Too handsome for his own good, some said. They claim Eli is the spitting image of him. The oldest boy favored Esther's side of the family, and she had a soft spot for him. But their father…" Fannie shook her head. "'Course, he died before Roman and I started courting."

"There was a tragedy with Eli's older brother, too, wasn't there?" Mam asked. "Terrible for your sister-in-law."

"And for Eli, I imagine." Ruth sprinkled sesame seeds over the coleslaw. She shivered at the thought of losing one of her sisters.

"It was Eli looking so much like his father that worried Esther," Fannie said. "At least that's what Roman thinks." She added more honey to her coffee. "Roman says Esther never gave the boy a chance to explain his side. You know, concerning that girl who made the accusations. Then, before the matter could be brought to the church, she took off—ran away."

It was on the tip of Ruth's tongue to ask Fannie if Roman had asked Eli himself if it was true about the girl, but she didn't. Maybe she didn't want to know? Maybe because as long as it was just a rumor, Ruth could think Eli might be innocent.

Mam shook her head. "Some English people think that such things never happen to us, but they do. We are all human and all capable of sin. It's what happens after we sin that really matters."

A knock on the door startled Ruth, and she crossed the kitchen to answer it.

"It's too early for Roman," Fannie said. "He…"

Ruth didn't hear the rest of what Fannie was saying. Her attention centered on the tall figure standing on the back porch. It was Eli. She swung open the door, suddenly feeling guilty. Had he heard them talking about him?

He grinned shyly. "Ruth."

"Eli." Her hands nervously found a speck of mayonnaise on her apron.

He stepped into the room. "I came early," he said, stating the obvious.

Eli's yellow hair was damp, his cheeks freshly shaved.

He was wearing English jeans and the Nittany Lions T-shirt, and his head was uncovered. No hat at all.

Mam rose from the table where the women had been enjoying their coffee. "Good to see you, Eli."

Eli shook his head. "I meant to say, I came early...to... speak to you," he said, directing his attention to Hannah.

Ruth looked at him. What he'd have to say to Mam, she couldn't imagine. Surely, he didn't have the nerve to ask if he could walk out with Miriam. Not dressed like that. And it was too soon. No one here really knew him. Surely, their mother wouldn't...

"Yes, what is it, Eli?" Ruth's mother didn't seem to notice the English clothes.

Eli straightened and cleared his throat. "They have movies," he began awkwardly. "At the mall."

"*Ya,*" Mam agreed. Her mouth tightened into a thin line, but her eyes twinkled with mischief. "This even I have heard."

Eli shuffled his feet. "Today, they show a..."

Ruth folded her arms over her chest. A movie at the mall? Her gaze darted from her mother back to Eli. He looked so young, so unsure of himself.

"Speak up," Fannie said.

His words came out in a rush. "A decent movie. *Noah and the Ark.* No bad talk or fancy behavior. I saw it. Last night. Roman and I went to be sure..."

Fannie's eyes widened in surprise. "That's where you and Roman went? He never said a word."

Eli extended one hand toward Hannah. "Would you give me permission to take—"

Mam frowned, interrupting. "You want to take my daughter to the mall? On a date?"

"Not a date, exactly. Just to see the movie. A good story, a Bible story. Educational. And full of wonders. The ark that God bade Noah to build, the animals, the great flood that covered the earth."

"Which one?"

Eli's brow furrowed beneath the fringe of yellow-blond hair. "Which one?"

"Which daughter do you wish to take?" Mam demanded, her eyes still twinkling.

"Um." His cheeks grew bright red. "Susanna and Anna, Miriam and Ruth."

"Oh, no," Ruth interrupted. "I'm not—" She fully intended to refuse the invitation but before she could get the words out of her mouth, she suddenly realized that she wanted to go. Desperately. With Eli. The back of her eyelids stung. But Eli had really come to ask Miriam to go to the show with him. He'd just asked about the rest of them when he had lost his nerve. He didn't really want Ruth to go. That was plain to see.

A slow smile spread over Mam's face. "And if Fannie and I wanted to go with you to see this *Noah and the Ark?* Would you take us as well?"

"Ya," Eli answered. "I would. And there would be room."

"On your motorbike?" Mam asked. She was teasing him outright now. Ruth knew it, and a small part of her felt sorry for Eli. Mam had raised his hopes. He looked so eager, and when Mam would tell him Miriam couldn't go, that none of them could go, he would be crushed.

"Ne." He raised his chin and stared back at her boldly. "I hoped you would let them go. I hoped they would want to, so I asked a driver to come with her van. There will be room for anyone who wants to go."

"Susanna would love it," Ruth put in, feeling a trickle of excitement.

"What of my dinner?" Mam asked. "What of my turkey and the ham?"

"There is a show at four o'clock," Eli explained. "We'll have time to eat, drive to the mall, see the movie, have an ice cream and be back before dark."

"I can see that you've thought this out," Mam said. She nibbled her bottom lip, a habit that Ruth and her mother shared. Then, Mam turned and looked straight at her. "What do you think, Ruth? Would your sisters like to see this movie?"

Fannie frowned. "The bishop might not think…"

"But the bishop isn't here. It's Ruth I asked," Mam said.

Ruth's mouth felt dry. "I think," she began. "I think that Miriam has not yet been baptized in the church, nor Susanna. I think the movie might be educational for them."

"And you?" Mam asked. "What do you think about going?"

Ruth couldn't look at her mother or Eli. She wanted to say she didn't want to go, but she couldn't lie.

"*Ya,* Mam," Ruth admitted glancing at the floor in front of Eli's boots. "I would like to see the movie, too."

"It's settled then." She nodded. "You may ask my girls, Eli. But I expect them home before dark."

"We will be," he promised. "I'll take good care of them."

"And one more thing," Mam said.

"Anything," Eli said.

"Church is here next week. I would like you to help us make ready. And I would like you to come to the services." She arched one eyebrow.

Eli grimaced. "I'll come because you ask," he said. "But don't blame me if your bishop kicks me out the door."

"He would never," Mam assured firmly. "Bishop Atlee is a fair man and a good shepherd to his flock. You'll be welcome here. You'll be welcome in our church, or I will know the reason why."

Anna, wearing her best Sunday-go-to-meeting dress and bonnet, led the way up the carpeted ramp through the darkened theater and found a seat. Ruth slid in beside her, followed by Susanna, clutching an enormous container of popcorn and so excited that she had the hiccups. Ruth had to admit it had been very thoughtful of Eli to invite Susanna. None of the boys in the neighborhood were unkind to Susanna, but Eli was the first to ask her to go on a date with her sisters.

Miriam sat on Susanna's right, leaving Eli next to the aisle. A few English turned to look and whisper, but then they lost interest and returned to their own conversations. Ruth could see that they were the only Amish in the movie this afternoon, perhaps in the mall. She had expected to be an object of curiosity, but stares always made her feel uneasy. She didn't think of herself as old-fashioned or quaint, simply apart from the larger world. The way she dressed and the way she lived was outward proof of a covenant with God; she didn't think herself better than the English, simply different. And different they were. That was obvious sitting here in the movie theater in a sea of brightly colored tank tops, dangling earrings and sparkly open-toed shoes.

Loud music blared from speakers on the walls, and on the screen, bottles of soda pop, boxes of candy and bags of popcorn danced and bounced. It looked very silly, but Susanna was entranced. She'd never seen a show before. Other than Eli, none of them had. Now that she was here, Ruth was nearly as excited as Susanna. She hoped that coming hadn't been wrong. It had always been a secret dream of hers to watch a movie in a real movie theater. There might be consequences next Sunday, but this afternoon, she would see one of the great stories of the Bible come alive.

Miriam was laughing and talking to Eli. They both seemed so much at ease here among the English, something Ruth had always struggled with. Of course, Eli wasn't wearing Plain clothing, but her sister was. Miriam's modest blue dress, black bonnet and apron and black shoes were as Plain as her own. Miriam always embraced new experiences wholeheartedly, and Ruth was certain that when it was the right time to join the church, she would be one of the most faithful. And if Eli and Miriam were to be a couple, he should realize that nothing would divide Miriam from her faith and family.

It wouldn't matter if Eli had done the terrible thing he'd been accused of, if he truly repented and made his peace with God and the church. Sometimes it was hard to forgive and forget bad sins, but forgiveness was an important part of their faith. How could a person expect God to forgive them their sins, if they were unable to forgive others? But Ruth doubted Mam would let this relationship between Miriam and Eli go much further without this serious matter being addressed.

The lights dimmed. A message appeared on the screen asking people to turn off their cell phones. But before that request had died away, Susanna leaned close and whispered that she needed to go to the bathroom. Ruth rolled her eyes. She'd known that giving Susanna a large soda pop was bound to have consequences. "I'll take her," Ruth whispered to Miriam.

When they returned, some sort of cartoon squirrel was scampering off the screen with a cupcake balanced on his head. A pit bull was chasing the squirrel but not having much luck, as the barking dog kept slipping in the strawberry icing. Susanna laughed and wiggled her way past Eli and Miriam back to her seat. Ruth followed. Then the music changed, and a rainbow of lights swirled on the big screen, signaling that the main feature was about to begin.

So entrancing was the story and so real were the characters playing Noah, his wife and their sons, that Ruth could almost, but not quite, forget that it was Miriam, not her, sitting beside Eli. Ruth was trying to concentrate on Noah's conversation with an invisible voice, when Eli passed Susanna another cup of soda pop. "You shouldn't give her…" But Susanna was already inhaling the drink. All that popcorn had made her thirsty all over again.

Eli shifted in his seat. The movie was a good one, better than the violent one he'd walked out of two weeks ago. He liked going to the theater. Usually, he sat near the back, by himself, and tried to understand the English, both on the screen and sitting around him. He and Hazel had sneaked away one night to see a romantic comedy. Both of them had been embarrassed by the loose behavior in the story. They'd stayed to the end, but he'd felt ashamed of himself as he'd walked out at the end of the feature. It had been wrong to bring Hazel there, and he knew it. But she'd wanted to go and had threatened to go with some of her girlfriends if he wouldn't take her.

Sometimes…most of the time…he felt as if he were caught halfway between the Plain life and the English world. He didn't know if he was completely responsible for Hazel's disgrace, but there was plenty of guilt to go around. Maybe she would have gotten into trouble even if he hadn't taken her to the party that night. He'd never know, and he'd never be sure if God or Hazel could ever forgive him. Because of their irresponsibility, a child had been conceived. Hazel's life, his life and the lives of their families might never be the same.

Did he have the right to be with another girl? A good girl like the sisters sitting beside him? Was he making another mistake, one he would live to regret? If he did choose the Amish path, would he later change his mind and run, as his father had?

Noah was leading the first pair of animals into the ark when Eli heard Susanna's whisper. This time, it was Miriam who took her hand and offered to escort her to the bathroom. Eli tensed. He swallowed, his mouth suddenly dry. When they returned, he could step out into the aisle and let Susanna and Miriam return to their seats. That was the right thing to do, the sensible thing.

But when the girls returned, Eli did what he'd wanted to do since they arrived; he got up, moved two seats over, and sat next to Ruth. She turned to look at him in surprise, before taking her elbow off the armrest dividing their seats and staring straight ahead at the screen.

Eli couldn't pay attention to the movie anymore. He was too acutely aware of the scent of green apple soap. The seats were very close, and he caught glimpses of Ruth's face in the flash of lightning from the screen. A feeling of protectiveness seeped up from the pit of his stomach. For all her prickly exterior, she was everything a man could ask for in a woman: beautiful, kind, strong-willed, loving. But she was more; Ruth was a true example of the faith. Why couldn't he have met her before he'd taken Hazel to that party? If he had…if he had, everything would be different. His life would be different now.

He locked his fingers together in his lap, and moisture rose along his collarbone. He didn't know what to do; he'd courted girls before, but no one like Ruth. He'd never felt this way about Hazel or Mary or Edith. He'd never worried that one of them might rebuff his attention. Maybe it would be better not to show Ruth how attracted he was to her, rather than make a fool of himself.

Eli glanced back at Miriam. She was leaning forward in her seat, deeply engaged in the movie. Susanna and Anna were both watching the movie screen, eyes wide with wonder. No one was watching him. No one would see him in the dark. Holding his breath, he reached over and covered Ruth's warm hand with his.

Startled, she turned toward him. For a second, her small hand trembled in his, as soft and fragile as a new-hatched chick....

In the dark, he searched her gaze and for just that split second, he felt a connection with her that he had never felt with anyone before. "Ruth."

His voice shattered the moment, and she pulled free. "Eli!" She looked at him and then away.

He felt his face grow hot with embarrassment. "I'm sorry. I didn't—"

"Shh," a woman called from the row behind them.

Anna glanced at Eli, then back at the screen.

Heart thudding against his ribs, Eli gave a sigh and turned back to the gathering storm that threatened to overturn the ark. He felt that way sometimes...lately, a lot of the time. But not tonight. Not tonight, because even though she had snatched her hand from his, she had let him hold it for a second, and he was pretty sure she had enjoyed it as much as he had.

With Ruth beside him here in the dark, peace and a sense of wonder settled over him. Whatever happened, nothing could take away his certainty that, at this moment in time, he was exactly where he should be.

Chapter Nine

On Tuesday morning, Ruth and Miriam took freshly picked strawberries, spinach, lettuce, radishes and twelve dozen eggs to Spence's. They rarely went to the auction on Tuesdays, but the strawberries might not keep until Friday's market. Both Anna and Susanna had remained at home to catch up on chores. There was a charity-work sewing bee at Aunt Martha's that night, and the four sisters and Mam would be going after a light supper.

As usual, Miriam drove the horse, and while she chatted merrily, Ruth just listened. What had happened at the movies had troubled her greatly—not only that Eli had attempted to hold her hand, but that she'd almost permitted it. Ruth grimaced. There was no getting around the truth. She had allowed him. It had only been for a few seconds, but she hadn't immediately pushed his hand away, and she couldn't deny that she'd felt a rush of excitement when his warm hand closed around hers.

And Anna had seen it. She hadn't mentioned it, but Ruth wasn't deceived. It simply wasn't Anna's way to intrude on personal matters or to chide her older sister for a serious breach of decorum. Eli's behavior afterward—pretending that nothing had happened and buying them all Boardwalk

Fries—only made things worse. Although she normally loved fries, Ruth hadn't been able to eat a bite. It would have choked her.

Eli was the worst sort of flirt. He'd taken Miriam to the movies, sat by her, and then tried to take liberties with another sister. It wasn't right. It just wasn't. Ruth didn't know what was allowed in *his* community, but it wasn't the way things were done *here*. As a baptized woman, Ruth should have known better than to go to the show with him at all. If she'd refused to attend the movie, if she'd protested, Mam might have kept her sisters home as well. But she hadn't. Eli had charmed her into forgetting who and what he was and who and what she was.

Then, to make matters worse, Ruth had been a coward afterward. She hadn't been brave enough to tell Miriam or her mother about the hand-holding incident. Instead, she'd acted as though everything was fine. She'd thanked Eli for taking them to the mall, and she'd told Mam about the movie and how tears had filled her eyes when the dove had returned to Noah with an olive leaf, proving that God's mercy had saved them from the flood. She'd laughed with Susanna about the monkeys riding on the tiger's back and the grumpy water buffalo. And all the time, in her heart, Ruth knew that she'd done something wrong…that she had committed a sin. The sin hadn't been the actual holding of hands, but the jealousy she had felt over Eli's attention to Miriam. And the pleasure she had taken, knowing he had held her hand for an instant, instead of Miriam's.

Ruth felt her face burn with shame. She wished she'd had the opportunity to talk to her mother, but Mam was busy with plans for Saturday's school picnic. They'd had to change the date so that the guests from the other churches could come. It would be a busy week when they added that on top of Sunday church at their house. For the picnic, each family with children in the school would bring food to share, but Mam always made extra dishes as well as treats for the children. There was so much to do this week that she just couldn't trouble Mam with her problems, especially those of her own making.

The traffic light changed; a truck horn blew, and Miriam flicked the leathers over Blackie's back. The horse trotted briskly through the busy intersection. Ahead were the railroad tracks. Spence's was only a few blocks away, and once they reached their stand, they might not get an opportunity to talk in private. Ruth opened her mouth, but before she could get a word out, Miriam asked. "All right. What's the matter? Did you catch Susanna's toothache?"

"What?"

Miriam chuckled. "You're as sour as one of *Grossmama's* pickles this morning."

"Am I?"

"*Ya.* You are." Miriam's brown eyes took on a concerned expression.

Ruth flushed an even brighter shade of red. Had Miriam seen Eli take her hand? Her pulse raced. "I'm not sure what we did Sunday was right."

Miriam laughed. "I thought so. You're feeling guilty about the show, aren't you? I thought it was wonderful. You can't tell me that you didn't have a good time."

"Movies are worldly. Not Plain."

"The story of Noah is from the Bible. I liked it. I'll go see it again, if I can convince Eli to take me."

"That's what I…" Ruth felt awkward. How could she say this? "Miriam, that's what I've been thinking about. I know you like Eli, but I'm afraid he isn't right for you," she blurted. "He…he's fast."

Miriam chuckled as the buggy bumped over the tracks. "He's not fast. He's just different from all the boys we know—the boys we've grown up with, and he's good-looking. That's why you're attracted to him." She glanced at Ruth. "You think he's cute, don't you?"

Ruth swallowed hard. "I'm not attracted to him. But he has a handsome face," she conceded.

"And nice shoulders." Miriam gave her a mischievous look. "Don't tell me you haven't noticed how wide his shoulders are. And he has nice hands."

More than that, Ruth thought. From the crown of his head to the soles of his feet, Eli was perfect. Just seeing him step into a room made her tongue stick to the roof of her mouth and her stomach do cartwheels. But good looks and a beautiful body were not what mattered most in choosing a husband. *For her sister.* What was important was the way a person was inside and if he shared your faith. An Amish marriage was about family and community and living according to God's word.

"Miriam, you're not listening to me. I'm trying to tell you that he may not be an appropriate beau for you."

Miriam laughed. "He's not *my* beau."

"But it looks like he's courting you. People think he is. And Eli isn't serious," Ruth insisted. "You can't trust him."

Miriam didn't say anything. She just kept sitting there with that silly smile on her face.

This wasn't going well at all. As much as Ruth loved Miriam, she could be so annoying, at times. She lowered her gaze, the guilt washing over her again. "There's something I have to tell you."

Another buggy was stopped ahead of them at the next light. Their cousin Dorcas leaned out of the carriage. "Hey," she called.

They waved back. "Do you think Dorcas is going to buy a pie at the market for tomorrow?" Miriam asked. "That might be smart if she wants to share pie with a boy on Saturday. The ones she bakes are even worse than yours." Miriam laughed, tickled with herself.

"I don't want to talk about Dorcas or about pies." Ruth clasped her hands together and hurried to confess what she'd done before she lost her nerve. "Miriam, listen to me. It was wrong, what Eli did," she finished. "He never should have tried to hold my hand when he was there with you."

"He held your hand?" Miriam cried excitedly.

"And I never should have let him. I'm so sorry, Miriam. It was wrong of me, I know, and—"

"That's what you've been so worried about for two days? Because Eli held your hand at the movies?" Miriam guided the horse around a produce truck that was double-parked in the street. Her voice was laced with amusement. "You should have said something. You've upset yourself for nothing. Eli isn't my boyfriend. He doesn't like me that way and I don't like him. I'm glad he held your hand."

"But—"

"When I find a boy I want to be with, I'll let him hold my hand. I might even let him kiss me. Once. After he asks me to be his wife, when I know he's serious. But before I gave him my answer." She looked at Ruth with great sincerity on her pretty face. "What if he's a bad kisser? Would you want a husband who was a bad kisser?"

Ruth was shocked. And relieved. Miriam didn't like Eli. She wasn't interested in him as a beau. "That's not the way to choose a husband, Miriam! You shouldn't be talking... even thinking about kissing."

"I think about kissing a lot," Miriam babbled on, not seeming to realize what a monumental moment this was for Ruth. If Miriam didn't like Eli, if he wasn't interested in Miriam, did that mean—

"What about Uncle Reuben?" Miriam continued with a giggle. "With that beard. It's so long and pointy. What kind of kisser do you think he is?"

"Miriam!"

Her sister grinned. "I'm just teasing you."

"Sometimes I wonder about you."

"Well, it's true. I will kiss my betrothed before we're married, and I won't feel guilty about it."

"Mam would be shocked if she heard you talk like that."

"Would she? For a happy marriage, you have to have love between a man and a woman. Then the tears and the laughter and the making of the children that follow will be right and good."

"I can't believe I misunderstood what was going on between you and Eli. I was so afraid you'd be upset with me, but you have to admit it would have been wrong to let Eli hold my hand if he was courting you."

"*Ya,* you're right. But if we were *walking out* together, and he would do such a thing, better for me to know before the wedding than after." Miriam guided Blackie off the street onto the gravel lane that ran behind the auction house.

"And you're sure Eli doesn't like you?" Ruth said.

"I think Eli is a special person. But he's not the one for me and I'm not the one for him. I think he's already set his sights on someone else. But that doesn't mean I can't have fun with him."

"People will think—"

"So long as Mam knows I'm doing right, so long as my family knows, I don't care about anyone else. Besides, I'm *rumspringa.* I plan to have some fun." She giggled. "But once I join the church, I'll be as upright as Johanna."

And they both laughed at the thought. Johanna was now

the ideal Amish mother and wife, but during her running around, their older sister had given Mam more than one sleepless night and more than one gray hair.

"Do you know what she said yesterday?" Miriam asked. "Johanna. About going to the picture show? She said that if she'd known we were going, she would have brought the baby and Jonah to Mam and come with us."

"Her husband would never have permitted it."

"Maybe not, but you know how headstrong she is." Miriam's eyes sparkled. "She takes after Mam."

"Mam?"

"Ya," Miriam answered. "Johanna told me that when Mam was a teenager, she used to go to the movies all the time with her English girlfriends."

"Do you think that's why she let us go?"

"Maybe she just wanted us to see for ourselves." Blackie trotted across the lot and came to a halt behind their usual table. "Good boy," Miriam said.

"Then I'm glad I went." Ruth got down from the buggy. "But I wouldn't have wanted to see a show that had shooting or bad language."

"Me, either." Miriam removed Blackie's bridle and slipped a halter over his head before tying him to a tree. They were lucky to have a table in the shade.

Feeling as if a great weight had been lifted off her shoulders, Ruth began to remove the boxes of strawberries. She had no idea how she felt about Eli or the hand-holding, now that she knew she hadn't interfered in Miriam's courting. At least she knew she hadn't hurt her sister. She had only the first tray out when a regular customer stopped and bought two dozen eggs and two quarts of berries. As Ruth counted out the change, she realized that they were short of dollar bills. "I'll go inside to the market," she offered. "As soon as we finish unloading."

"Need some help?"

Ruth turned to see Eli standing behind her.

She glanced at Miriam in confusion. He was the last person she wanted to see today. What should she say to him? She didn't look at him; her hands trembled as she tucked the change into the little cloth pouch they kept it in. "Shouldn't you be at the shop?" she blurted.

"Roman had some refinished furniture to be auctioned off today. I brought it in, and I'll wait to collect his money." Eli pulled eggs from under the buggy seat and carried them to the table.

"Good," Miriam said, plucking the money bag from Ruth's hand. "Since Eli's here to help, I'll go get that change."

"Don't go," Ruth said. "Eli's not..." But her sister was already walking away. Ruth glanced at Eli, and he grinned back at her.

"Guess you're stuck with me."

"I don't need any help." She tried hard not to look into his eyes.

A tattooed woman with long white-blond hair and short shorts waved her hand at Ruth. "Miss! Can I get some service here? Are these local strawberries?"

"Picked this morning," Eli assured her. Flashing a big smile, he grabbed up a plastic bag and went to the table. "You won't find any fresher. Or sweeter. How many quarts would you like?"

A bald man with a little dog on a leash approached the table. Ruth sold him radishes, lettuce and a dozen eggs. Two more customers stopped, and Eli went back to the buggy to bring more strawberries as Ruth waited on them. Business was brisk for ten minutes, and Ruth would have run short of change, but Eli changed a twenty for her with small bills from his pocket.

"Are you thirsty?" he asked when there was a break. "Would you like a soda pop?"

She shook her head. "I'm not thirsty."

He was standing so close that his gaze made her nervous...made her remember when he'd tried to hold her hand. She felt herself blush. "Thank you for your help. I'm sure you have things to do. There's no need for you—"

"I like helping you. I think we make a good pair, don't you? Look, half your berries are gone already. You'll be sold out before noon." He grinned. "Unless you want to stick around and let me buy you lunch."

She shook her head adamantly. "No. Miriam and I have to go home. We have to finish chores and start supper. There's a work bee tonight at Aunt Martha's."

"I know. The men are going. We're repairing Reuben's windmill."

Ruth tried to think of something to say that wouldn't sound stupid but she couldn't think of anything. She straightened the rows of quarts of berries.

Eli leaned against the table and crossed his arms over his chest; he'd pushed up his sleeves so his muscular forearms flexed. "Are you baking a pie for the school picnic?"

"I suppose."

His blue eyes danced with mischief. "Do you make good pies?"

"Not very good," she admitted. She couldn't help smiling. "Awful, as a matter of fact."

An English woman pushing a baby stroller approached. "Are your eggs fresh?" she asked Eli.

"Still warm from the hen," he quipped.

Ruth nibbled her lower lip. How could he talk to the English so easily? She felt a twinge of uneasiness and glanced up to see Aunt Martha glaring at her from her stand across the way.

"How much are your berries?" the woman customer asked, ignoring the sign. "That other stand usually has them cheaper."

"They do sell them cheaper," Eli said. "But ours are larger and haven't been sitting in a refrigerator since last week." He winked at Ruth, completely embarrassing her. But a part of her liked it.

The woman nodded and picked up two quarts.

Most of Aunt Martha's strawberries were still on her table. She wouldn't be pleased if Ruth sold out first. "Maybe I should go and see if Miriam's all right," Ruth suggested when the lady pushed her stroller away, carrying the strawberries.

"I'm sure she's fine. You can't leave me. More people may come, and then it will take both of us. The English, they hate to wait." He pushed his wide-brimmed hat a little higher and smiled at her. "After all, this is your stand. You wouldn't want to leave me to do all the work, would you? Besides, I make a mistake and then they'd be buying from your aunt Martha next time." He rolled his eyes.

Ruth couldn't help herself. She smiled back.

"It took forever, and by the time I got back, Eli and Ruth had sold all the strawberries," Miriam chattered. "Can you believe that?" She dropped the handle of the red wagon. "Your turn, Ruth. This is halfway."

The evening was so nice that Miriam had suggested the five of them walk to Aunt Martha's. The shortest way wasn't by the road but through the apple orchard, down the woods trail and across Uncle Reuben's meadow.

"All them strawberries," Susanna echoed. She was wearing a new robin's-egg-blue dress tonight and was so pleased with herself that she kept hopping from one foot to the other.

"What Miriam's not telling you is that she abandoned me," Ruth teased. With a mock sigh, she picked up the handle of the child's high-sided wagon. She would need to take care not to turn it over in the sandy lane and spill the treats they were bringing to share. As usual, Anna had used her time wisely, and the cookies and molasses doughnuts had already been made when they got home from the sale. The wooden wagon was even heavier to pull this evening because Mam had insisted on bringing three pounds of butter, a gallon of buttermilk and four quarts of strawberries. What Aunt Martha needed with more strawberries, Ruth didn't know, but it was one of those instances when it was easier to go along with Mam than to argue with her.

"Can't you walk faster?" Anna asked. "We'll be late for the prayer."

"Go on ahead," Ruth said. "Aunt Martha will be put out if she has to wait." She didn't mind pulling the wagon. Anna had done all the baking today, and it was a beautiful night for a walk. Birds were singing in the apple trees; frogs were croaking, and the air smelled sweetly of honeysuckle. "If I'm late, I'll just sneak in the back."

"Maybe we should go ahead," Mam agreed. She stopped beneath the spreading branches of an apple tree. "But I have something I need to talk to you about first, girls. It's Irwin. Samuel said that the board members have been getting complaints from parents. Some of the other children are saying Irwin started the fire at the schoolhouse. If anyone brings it up tonight, say nothing that will contribute to the gossip."

"What a terrible thing to accuse him of," Anna exclaimed.

Miriam considered the accusation. "The poor boy is ornery, but setting the school on fire?"

Ruth looked at her sisters, then at Mam. She wished she

could tell Miriam and Anna about seeing Irwin running from the school after the fire broke out, but she'd promised Mam not to tell anyone. As time passed, as difficult as it was to believe that the boy would do such a terrible thing, there were no other suspects, and it seemed as though he might be guilty. And if he was, she didn't know what would happen. Someone who started fires was dangerous. She hoped that no one would bring in the English police. No matter how serious, it was better to keep Amish trouble in the community.

"I'm not ready to give up on Irwin," Mam said. "I don't want any of you to, either. I talked to Lydia today and I've arranged for Irwin to come to our place early before school and again in the afternoons to help with the milking and outside chores."

"You want Irwin near our cows?" Miriam asked. "After he let them into the corn?"

"Mam, I don't think—" Anna began.

"It's settled, girls. It will be good to have a man around the farm again." Mam chuckled. "Even a beanpole of a boy, badly in need of fattening up."

"But Miriam and Ruth milk the cows," Susanna said.

"There's plenty of work for all of us," Mam assured her. "And I know I can count on all of you to be kind and make Irwin welcome."

It took a great deal of effort for Ruth to hold her tongue, but she stared at the ground and kept walking slowly as the others hurried on ahead and vanished down the lane.

Of all of her mother's ideas, this one with Irwin had to be the worst. Ruth jerked the wagon over the ruts in the dirt lane. What if the boy started a fire at their place? They'd have to watch him closely, and from what she'd seen of Irwin, he'd be a lot more trouble than he was worth.

The left wheel suddenly sank into the sand and the

wagon tilted. Ruth dropped the handle and grabbed the glass jar of buttermilk with one hand and the toppling basket of gingerbread with the other. Strawberries rolled out onto the ground. "Christmas fudge!" she cried.

"What kind of talk is that?" came a voice out of the rows of apple trees to her left.

Ruth knew that voice. She twisted around to see Eli coming toward her out of the trees. "Stop that," she snapped.

"Stop what?"

"Sneaking up on me. You keep doing that!"

He laughed. "It looks like you need help, Ruth Yoder. Unless you want me to keep walking and leave you to deal with this all by yourself." He scooped up a strawberry, blew the sand off and popped it into his mouth.

"What are you doing here?" She felt foolish. Again. She was down on her knees trying to rescue Anna's cookies and the gingerbread, both in danger of following the errant berries. "Don't just stand there. Grab something."

Eli took hold of the corner of the wagon and lifted it. The jar of buttermilk, the strawberries and the desserts slid back to safety. Ruth got to her feet and brushed the dirt off her dress. "You're lucky I came when I did," he said. "Otherwise." Eli shrugged. "Gingerbread disaster."

"This isn't the quickest way from Roman's to Aunt Martha's house."

He looked solemn. "It's not? That's funny. Miriam told me to come this way."

"Miriam? Did you think she'd be walking along this lane this evening?"

"I'll never tell." He folded his arms over his chest.

Ruth was almost sure he was teasing her. Had Miriam planned this? It was her idea that they should walk. She took the first turn with the wagon, not sure whether or not she liked the idea that he planned to come this way just so he could bump into her. She had a mind to send him on his way. But the wagon was heavy and they were going the same way. She exhaled. "So long as you're here, you may as well pull the wagon."

"Ya," he agreed. "That might be best." He was laughing at her with his eyes, enjoying getting her goat once again.

She watched him as he grabbed the handle of the wagon. "Why do you do this?"

"What? Come to your rescue all the time?"

She made a sound of exasperation, but it came out lame even to her ears. "Stop teasing me."

"I like teasing you. It's just too easy."

"Fine. Be like that." She turned and started walking down the lane, leaving him to follow with the wagon. Her heart was racing. She felt giddy. And it was all his fault.

"Ruth."

The sound of her name on his lips was as sweet as the mockingbird's song. She glanced back at him.

"Will you walk with me?" He wasn't teasing her now. His tone was sincere. His gaze held hers.

"Why should I?" She was asking herself as much as him.

He stopped and pushed his wide-brimmed hat up, and she found herself looking right into his blue eyes.

"Please," he said.

She felt suddenly breathless. "If you want," she answered softly. "But talk only. No more holding of hands."

"Ne," he said. "Of course not." But he couldn't leave it at that. "Not unless you want to."

"Why should I want to hold your hand?"

"I don't know. I think maybe you wanted me to before."

"I did not."

He laughed, walking beside her. "I don't take you for a liar, Ruth. It's one of the reasons I like you. I would think you would always be honest with people."

How can he know that? she wondered. *I can't even always be honest with myself.* But he was right, she couldn't out-and-out lie. "Okay, maybe I wanted you to, a little. Maybe," she admitted. "But it was a mistake."

"*Ya,*" he agreed. "Probably a mistake, but nice. Very nice."

Chapter Ten

Walking beside Ruth felt good to Eli. For all her prickly exterior, there was something so sweet and innocent about her that it made him want to throw his arms in the air and shout for joy. And what he said about thinking she would not lie was true, even if he had been teasing her. What he liked about Ruth was that she wore her faith, not like a crown of thorns, but as a glittering mantle of content. She knew who she was, and she liked the person she was. She believed in herself and God. She didn't have to preach to people. Simply watching her as she followed the righteous path, day after day, made him wish he was the kind of man Ruth would choose to marry.

Since the death of his brother, he'd drifted further and further from the Amish way of life. The incident with Hazel had alienated him even more from his community, and the notion that he'd never be able to find his way back haunted his dreams. Was he too much like his father, as his mother had accused? Was it impossible for him to consider living in the faith he'd been born into?

If he'd taken Hazel to be his wife as everyone had expected, assumed responsibility for her child and formally asked for forgiveness, there would be no question of his future. He could have taken over his grandfather's wood-working shop and made a decent living building sturdy kitchen cabinets, lawn furniture and storage sheds. His community would have embraced him, and in time, the gossip would have faded and his new family would have been accepted.

But, as much as he'd liked Hazel, he hadn't loved her. He hadn't been able to turn his back on the possibility that he'd find a girl he truly loved and marry her. And he hadn't wanted to spend the rest of his life making lawn furniture. He wanted to shape beautiful things out of wood, to bring the images in his head to shape, to make his birds come alive. Selfishly, he'd put his own desires before the needs of the baby and Hazel. And now, things might never be made right.

Eli was afraid he hadn't changed, and he hadn't learned from his mistakes. Proof that he was still acting selfishly was right here in this apple orchard. Instead of involving Ruth in his troubles, he should get on his scooter and drive to the far end of the country, perhaps even to Alaska. He should go where no one knew him and where no Amish had settled. He should find a place where being Plain meant nothing to the English, and Eli Lapp would be just another craftsman who was skilled with wood.

Instead, he was walking through an apple orchard with the most fascinating woman he'd ever met, a devoted daughter and sister whom he had no chance of winning, someone who would someday marry a God-fearing Plain man. Together, the two of them would raise a family of red-cheeked, happy kids, children who would know who and where they belonged and would never imagine turning English. *Ruth.* Even her name was straight from the pages of the holy book. It was Ruth who sacrificed everything for love. He would never deserve her; he was causing trouble for her just by being near her.

But he couldn't make himself let go.

Eli thought that if he could explain what had happened with Hazel to anyone, he would like it to be Ruth. And he needed to talk to someone about it. It was like a burr in his shoe, always there, always rubbing. He knew Ruth had heard the rumors, and it was unfair to keep the truth from her. But he had to protect Hazel, and dragging her down to excuse his own actions would be a worse sin than what he'd done, wouldn't it?

"Eli."

A flood of emotion swelled in his chest. *"Ya?"*

Was it right that he could take such pleasure in hearing her say his name? He was like any other man, English or Amish, but Ruth was special. He'd never felt so happy just to walk with a girl. He remembered how warm and soft her small hand had felt, and how right it had felt, sitting in the semidarkness of the movie theater beside her.

"Are you coming to church tomorrow at our house?" she asked, breaking through his thoughts.

He didn't want to. It would be a mistake. Sitting through the sermon, letting himself believe that there might be hope for him and then having that hope dashed. It would simply hurt too much.

"Are you?" she pressed when he didn't answer.

"I promised your mother, didn't I?" he hedged. Not that it would be of any use. He'd leave the service with the same empty feeling he'd had for years, that he wasn't worthy of God's love…that he didn't belong.

"You should come. Mam will be disappointed if you don't." She turned to look into his eyes. "But you have to want to be there. It's no good if you sit like a lump or let your mind wander. You have to open your heart to the preacher's message."

"What if it's not meant for me?" he asked, revealing more than he wanted to, more than was safe.

"But it is," she insisted. "We have only to believe in our faith, to follow the laws, and we're assured of a place in heaven."

"You, maybe. Being good comes easy for you."

"*Ne*. That's not true." There was a little smile at the corners of her mouth as she looked down at her bare feet. "You don't really know me. I'm selfish and impatient. I judge people too quickly, and…" She sighed. "This list is long. I work at it every day. I really do. But I have failures and doubts. Everyone does. Like with Irwin."

"What's he doing now? More trouble?"

She shook her head. "Mam asked me not to talk about it…but…she wants him to come and help us out on a regular basis. I don't know if it's safe to have him on our farm. When I saw the fire at the schoolhouse…"

He waited, unwilling to press her.

"You can't say anything," she told him, obviously hesitant.

He stopped the wagon. "You know I won't. What is it, Ruth? What's troubling you? What did you see?" She was close enough for him to smell the clean scent of her hair and see the concern in her dark brown eyes.

"He crawled out from under the cloakroom and ran away. And he had burns on his hands."

"You think he started the fire?"

She nodded. "Mam says not to jump to conclusions until we know, but Irwin won't ever tell us if he's guilty. He never admits to doing wrong. I know he's been hurt by losing his family, but what if there had been children inside the classroom? They could have been killed. Setting fires is not just a boy's mischief. It's evil."

Eli let go of the wagon handle and folded his arms over his chest. "Have you asked Irwin what happened?"

Ruth rolled her eyes. "I can't get two words out of him. Samuel's twins may know something, but they aren't talking, either."

"What if I talk to the boys, see what I can find out? Maybe it would be different coming from me, me being a bad boy and all."

He smiled and she smiled back. A smile that lit up his heart.

"I'd appreciate it," Ruth said with a nod. "Mam has a good heart, but…"

"She's a wise woman."

"I'm afraid she's too trusting."

A high-pitched yelp broke the tranquility of the twilight. Eli glanced around, trying to find the source. "Did you hear that?"

"Over there." Ruth pointed toward a hedgerow at the edge of the orchard. "I think it's some kind of animal. Maybe a fox."

The pitiful squeal came again. A thick wall of mulberry bushes and old-growth cedar trees ran along the property line between the Yoder farm and that of Martha and Reuben Coblentz. Eli left the wagon, and as he approached the hedgerow, sparrows flew up out of the wild roses. He crouched down and carefully pushed aside the thorny foliage.

"Be careful," Ruth cautioned. She had followed him, but stayed back. "It might be a sick raccoon. You know they can carry rabies."

Something thrashed in the prickly vines. "What's wrong? Are you hurt?" he murmured and then laughed.

"Well, look at this." He thrust his hand into the tangle and pulled out a ragged, burr-encrusted and pitifully thin puppy. "It's a dog," he announced.

Half-healed cuts and patches of dried blood marred the little animal's black-and-white fur. One paw was swollen and the plume of a tail so matted that it was hard to see where briars ended and puppy began. One ragged ear stood up and one hung down, but black button eyes stared at him hopefully and a red tongue licked at his hand. The whine rose to a joyous yip, and the little dog wriggled so hard Eli thought it might pop out of its skin.

"Ach," he said. "You've had a rough time of it, haven't you?"

"Oh, let me see," Ruth cried. "Poor little baby. How did he get here?"

"Probably dumped by the English." Eli stood. "It happened all the time on my grandfather's farm. City people think they can just drop their animals in the country."

"Poor baby. Let me hold him."

"Better not," he cautioned. "He's crawling with fleas."

She uttered a sound of amusement. "Think I'm afraid of a few fleas? Give him to me." She took the puppy from his hands and held it against her. "Sh, sh, hush now, *liebchen*. You're safe now," she crooned. "We'll take care of you."

The puppy began sucking frantically at her fingertips.

"He's hungry."

"Starving, I'd say. He was caught in the briars. He may have been out here for days."

"Poor little thing." She looked up at Eli, her brown eyes sparkling with determination. "I'm going to take him home and feed him."

"He needs a bath, I'd say."

"First some chicken broth and rice, then a bath." She

glanced back at the wagon full of goodies. "Can you take those things to Mam? I'll have to miss tonight's work bee. I can't take him with me, and he needs attention now."

"You're willing to miss the frolic to tend to a stray?"

She laughed, heading back toward the path. "It wouldn't be the first time."

"It's too small to be of much use as a farm dog. There must be an animal rescue place in Dover." He followed her. "I could take it there tomorrow if you want."

"Ne." She shook her head. "We found him, Eli. God must want us to take care of him."

He thought about that. He liked animals, but his grandfather had never allowed any animal on the farm that wasn't of use, either for work or meat. Old horses and cows past their prime had gone to the auction, and barn kittens had regularly been disposed of. As a child, he'd shed tears when a favorite was sold off or simply vanished, but he'd learned to accept the way things were.

Ruth's determination to care for this little waif touched him. "If you're going to take the dog home, I could deliver the food and then come back to help—"

"Ne." She shook her head. "It would not look right, both of us missing. People would think that we were together."

He smiled at her in what he hoped was a persuasive way. "But that would be true, wouldn't it? We would be together, taking care of the pup."

"Are you looking for a way to get out of work? Uncle Reuben expects you to do your share." She looked down at the squirming dog in her arms. "I can do this. You just take Mam's contributions to the house."

"You're sure?"

"I'm sure."

"What will your mother say about you bringing him

home?" he ventured. He knew what his mother or his grandmother would have said. *The dog wasn't worth saving.*

Ruth smiled up at him and then turned away, headed back toward her farm. "She'll fuss at the cost of the shots and vet bills, but she'll let me keep him. Mam only pretends to be tough. Inside, she's as soft as Susanna's whoopie pie filling." She looked back over her shoulder at him. "Good night, Eli Lapp. See you another day."

"Another day," he murmured to himself. The he grabbed the wagon handle and hurried up the lane. He couldn't wait for another day with Ruth.

"Women are in the front room," Reuben said, not seeming to care why Eli was pulling the Yoders' wagon. "Just carry that stuff in and leave it on the kitchen counter. Then come back and find a hammer. There's some loose nails on the windmill ladder. You can start by fixing that."

Eli nodded and picked up the gallon jar of buttermilk. It had gathered a little dust but otherwise seemed none the worse for wear. Taking the gingerbread in his free hand, he walked up onto the screened porch and into the kitchen. Every available tabletop and counter seemed to be crammed with food, but he found a spot and slid the buttermilk into the open space.

From thc other room, he heard the murmur of chattering women. But as he turned back to fetch the rest of Hannah's things, he caught snatches of conversation coming from the porch.

"...asking for trouble. If my brother was alive, this would never happen." A hand pulled the screened door open.

"But he's not. And I have to do what I think is—" Hannah stopped in mid-sentence and smiled at Eli. "I saw the wagon. Is Ruth inside?"

Eli shook his head. "We found an abandoned puppy in the hedgerow. It was hurt. She took it back to the farm."

"What? A dog?" the older woman said. "I never."

"This is Reuben's Martha," Hannah said, introducing them.

He nodded. "You have the stand across from the Yoders, at Spence's."

Martha sniffed and scowled at him.

"It was good of you to bring the food." Hannah glanced at her sister-in-law. "Susanna picked you some more strawberries. I know you said you wanted to make more jam. Where would you like Eli to put them?"

"In the milk house." Martha pointed. "Over there. There's a cold box, set into the ground." Her mouth tightened into a thin line. "You're late. The men have already started work."

Eli stepped aside to let them pass. Had they been talking about him?

"It's time your Ruth was married, and the next two as well," Martha went on as they walked by. "They come and go as they please."

Eli hurried out onto the porch, eager to get away from the disagreeable woman, but not before he heard her add, "You're treading on thin ice, Hannah. You'll be lucky if you're not reprimanded by the bishop for running such a loose household."

Hannah's soft voice carried through the open window. "You mean well, sister, but you're too quick to judge."

"Are you accusing me of…"

Eli took the porch steps two at a time and let out a breath of relief when he saw Tyler coming across the yard. "Hey," Eli called to him. "Take these cookies inside and the strawberries to the milk house. Reuben is waiting on me."

"Cookies? Sure." Tyler motioned toward the side of the house. "The guys are all over by the windmill."

Eli headed in that direction. He'd take Ruth's wagon home later, once the work was done. Nothing would get him back in Martha's house tonight, or ever again, if he could at all help it. In the distance, he heard male laughter and the sound of hammering. Feeling guilty about the harm he might have done to Ruth's reputation, he quickened his steps.

It was almost eleven when Eli approached Ruth's back porch with the wagon. Only one light was burning up on the second floor, so he tried not to make any more noise than necessary. A few yards from the house stood an old-fashioned, covered well with a winch and bucket and a peaked cedar roof that extended out about three feet. Eli stowed the wagon there. It had clouded up and looked as though it might rain before morning. He didn't want to leave the wooden wagon where it might get wet.

He was still feeling guilty about the confrontation he'd overheard between Hannah and Martha, so he wasn't concentrating on where he was going. As he turned to go, he stumbled over a second bucket in the dark. "Ouch!" he cried.

"Clumsy," came a female voice from the darkness.

He turned and squinted toward the dark house. "Ruth?"

"Did you hurt yourself?" He spotted movement. She was sitting on the porch swing.

"*Ne.*" He had slammed his shoulder into the brick wall surrounding the well, but he was too embarrassed to say so. "I thought you'd turned in."

"Shh. Mam and my sisters are already asleep."

He went to the porch, resting one foot on the first step, but made no move to join her. "How's the dog?"

"Jeremiah. I'm going to call him Jeremiah."

"More name than dog."

She laughed, and she patted the seat beside her on the swing. "Want to see?"

The dog lay curled in her lap, fast asleep.

Knowing he was probably making a big mistake, Eli crossed the porch and sat on the other end of the porch swing. Though old, it was a nice swing. Well built. He wondered if her father had made it. Roman said Jonas Yoder had been a solid craftsman, well respected by both the Amish and English. "I think I might have caused trouble for your mother tonight."

"Aunt Martha?"

"How did you guess?"

Ruth gave the swing a push.

"I don't want to cause trouble for your family."

"Aunt Martha doesn't think Mam should have Irwin working for us. She made such a fuss at the bee that Lydia started to cry."

"So it wasn't me?"

"My cousin Dorcas did tell Mam that you were working at our stand on Tuesday. Luckily, Miriam and I had already told her." Ruth's voice flowed as sweet as honey in the soft darkness of the moist evening air. She held out a towel-wrapped bundle. "I gave him a bath. He smells a lot better."

Eli took the dog awkwardly. "I don't think your uncle likes me much, either."

"Uncle Reuben? He's all right. He takes being a preacher seriously, but he's not mean. And sometimes his sermons are good. Too long, but good. You're lucky. Sunday, we have a guest minister from Virginia. He's visited before, and he doesn't preach nearly as long. And he's funny. He always works jokes in. But you remember the stories he tells from the Bible. His name is David Miller. Do you know him?"

"*Ne*. At home, we mostly had visitors from Lancaster. Bishops and preachers, that is. Regular visitors from all over the country."

"Same here," Ruth said.

The puppy whimpered in his sleep, and Eli petted him. You could feel every bony little rib, but his belly was extended and warm. "He ate good?"

"Mam said I gave him too much, but he was so hungry." She gave the swing another push. "Are you fooling with me, Eli?"

He swallowed. "What?"

"Tell me the truth. I thought you liked Miriam."

"*Ne*. I mean, I do, but not like that. Not as a girlfriend."

"Oh." Her voice was thoughtful, but he couldn't tell what she was thinking.

"I thought you did," she said.

"It's you I like, Ruth." He watched her in the dark, surprised by his own boldness. He was taking a chance being honest with her, telling her how he felt, but he needed to say it. "Just you."

She didn't answer.

He stroked the sleeping puppy. "A lot. I like you a lot."

"But you always talked to her."

"Miriam's fun. Why shouldn't I talk to her? Besides, *you* wouldn't talk to me."

She was quiet for a minute, and he could tell she was thinking. That was something he liked about Ruth. She was smart. She thought before she spoke, unlike him. It always seemed as if he was saying dumb things.

"You scare me, Eli. I don't know what to think."

"*Ya,*" he agreed. "You scare me, too."

Chapter Eleven

Eli reached for her hand, but she drew it away.

"Things are too complicated."

"Because of what people say about me?"

She drew in a long breath.

The air was warm. Frogs and insects chirped and buzzed in the soft night. The air smelled of flowers and newly mown grass. Eli felt as though he would fly apart at any second, burst into splinters. He wanted this girl more than anything, more than he'd wanted his mother when she sent him away as a child...more than he wanted to fashion beautiful furniture out of seasoned hardwood. "Ruth."

"Shh, hear me out," she murmured. "You have to understand. I can't be selfish. I have to do what is right."

"Maybe us meeting is right...is what we are supposed to do." She was so near. He felt big and clumsy. His palm ached to enfold hers. All he wanted was to touch her hand. "I've done things I shouldn't have. But I'd never do anything to hurt you."

"I have to think, to decide what is best." She toyed with the undone string on her *Kapp*. "If I did leave Mam... leave my home...it could only be with a baptized man who shared my faith, who could give his life to God, who could follow our rules. Do you understand?"

"I wish I was as sure of God's will as you are," he admitted.

"I wish you were, too." She rose to her feet. "I have to go in."

"Can I see you again? Can we *walk out* together?"

"I don't know, Eli. I have to pray on it. It's a big step. I've always thought to stay with Mam and Susanna. I can't just change my mind without considering what that would mean." She took a few steps and then turned and reached out for the sleeping puppy. "I'd like to be your friend, no matter what."

He ran a hand through his hair. "I don't know if that's possible, if I could be just…just your friend. Or…" A weight crushed his chest. "Or, if I can ever find the faith you have."

"Pray on it," she advised. "It always helps."

"I'll try."

She cradled the dog in her arms. "Jeremiah is just the right name for him, don't you think?"

He didn't answer, and she slipped into the house, leaving him alone on the porch swing. He sat there for nearly an hour, wishing he could be the man she wanted, wishing she was still here beside him in the soft spring night.

"You should have been there," Anna said, mounding a deep bowl of flaky pie dough into a ball. "Aunt Martha made such a fuss about Irwin."

"Enough of such talk," Mam warned. "She only means the best for us. Her heart is good." It was late on Friday afternoon, and they had gathered in the kitchen to bake pies and prepare food for the school picnic.

Even Johanna had come to help, bringing three-year-old Jonah and the baby.

"You think everyone's heart is good, Mam," Ruth said.

"Amen to that," Miriam agreed. The rest of them laughed.

Mam had received letters from Rebecca and Leah today. Leah's letter was short and funny, but Rebecca had filled them in at great length on all the doings at *Grossmama's* house and in the church and community. It was easy to see why she was a regular contributor to the *Budget*.

"Be careful," Susanna said to Jonah. She was rocking Baby Katie and keeping a watchful eye on Johanna's son as he petted the puppy. "You have to be gentle with him."

"I am," Jonah declared. "I am, isn't I?"

"You are, and I'm proud of you." Johanna beamed at Susanna. "You're so good with both of them," she said. "I wish I had you at my house all the time."

"She has the touch," Anna said, as she tore off a section of dough and dropped it onto a floured board.

Ruth passed her sister a rolling pin. Her own piecrust was as flat and round as she could get it. The dough had already torn twice, and she knew that she'd probably make it worse when she tried to get it into the pie pan. She could make decent biscuits and muffins. Why was pie always a disaster for her? Her crusts were so tough that even Mam teased her that they could patch the holes in the orchard lane with them.

"What's this I hear about someone sitting on our porch swing in the wee hours of the night this week?" Johanna asked. She looked especially sweet today in a lavender dress and white apron. She'd left her shoes on the porch and was barefoot like the rest of them.

"It wasn't someone," Susanna said. "It was Eli. He

was on the porch with Roofie and Jeremiah. They were swinging."

"Talking," Ruth corrected. "We were talking."

Anna giggled. "Wouldn't Aunt Martha love to know that? She'd scorch your ears after church." She wiped floured hands on her apron. "Ach! Mam, the pies. Are they burning?"

"I wouldn't be surprised," Mam said. "More chatter than work, I'd say."

Ruth grabbed a towel and used it to shield her hands from the heat as she opened the oven door on the woodstove and began to remove Miriam's and Mam's pies. "Perfect."

"Don't say that yet," Miriam warned. "You haven't tasted them."

The kitchen door opened, and Irwin stuck his head in. A battered straw hat with an Ohio-style brim hid his pale face. "I got eggs."

Mam waved him in. "Put the eggs on the table. Let me see what you have."

Eyes downcast, Irwin ventured into the warm kitchen and did as he was told. For the past two days, he'd come after school to help with the outside chores, but as far as Ruth was concerned, the boy was lazy. The only thing he'd shown interest in was eating and staring at the new puppy. "Did you clean out the chicken waterers and fill them with fresh water?" she asked. Yesterday he'd forgotten, and she and Miriam had had to do it.

Irwin nodded and nudged Jeremiah with one dirty foot. The trace of a smile skimmed over his thin lips before vanishing behind an expressionless mask. "Can I hold him?"

Ruth blinked as she deposited the last pie safely on the stovetop. Irwin never spoke to Mam unless he was forced to. "Jeremiah's not strong enough to play yet," she said.

"Maybe when he's put on some weight and his cuts have healed."

"I know about dogs," Irwin said. "I had me one. Her name was Gretel."

"Where is she?" Susanna asked. "I love dogs."

"Smoke got her."

"Smoke?" Susanna's freckled nose wrinkled. "How did smoke get her?"

"Was it the fire that killed your family?" Ruth asked.

"Yep. Would have got me, too, but I wasn't home that night." He crouched down and stroked the skinny pup. "Gretel was a smart dog. She followed me to school every day. She could sit up and beg and roll over. Better than your dumb dog."

Irwin's thin voice cracked and lower lip quivered.

It was all Ruth could do to keep from weeping. This boy had lost everything in one terrible night, and she'd been less than charitable toward him. He was as damaged inside as Jeremiah was on the outside. No wonder Irwin acted out.

"I think we could use your help in training Jeremiah," Mam said brusquely. "We haven't had a puppy in a long time, and most dogs will learn quicker from a man."

Johanna turned her face away and stifled a giggle. Mam glanced at Ruth, and she understood that her mother was slicing the truth thin to soothe Irwin's pride.

"You may hold Jeremiah, if you are careful," Mam added. "After you've finished with the eggs."

"Wash your hands," Ruth said. "Take these eggs back on the porch and clean them with the vinegar rag. Put the cracked ones aside in the tin bowl, so Miriam can cook them for the pigs. Dry the perfect eggs and put them in the cartons."

"I break stuff," Irwin said. "Maybe somebody else should wash the eggs."

"No," Mam said. "We all learn best by doing. I'm depending on you to do your best. The egg money is important to us. When you're done, you can take care of the puppy. We're busy today, and I think he needs the attention."

"Me want to help Ir'n!" Jonah scrambled to his feet. "Me can wash eggs."

Miriam rolled her eyes. Ruth chuckled as she wondered how many dozen would survive to make it to market next week. "I'm going to watch to see you do it right," Ruth said. She thought Jonah and Jeremiah would be safe from Irwin's mischief, but she was going to keep a sharp eye out for trouble.

"So...you sat on the porch swing with the Belleville boy," Johanna said, when Jonah and Irwin had left the kitchen. "Anything more we should know?"

"Ne," Ruth said, more sharply than she intended. She didn't want to think about Eli, let alone talk about him in front of Mam and her sisters. She didn't know her own mind yet. "We're just friends."

Anna chuckled. "Where have I heard that before?"

Mam watched through the screen door as the boys washed and dried the eggs. How many were lost, Ruth didn't want to guess, but Jonah seemed none the worse for wear when they returned to the kitchen.

"I can hold Jeremiah now," Irwin said.

"You can," Ruth agreed. "Gently."

"Gentle," Jonah echoed. He stared up at Irwin with all the awe of a small boy for a bigger one. "He little." And then, he repeated, "Jeremiah little."

"I know." Irwin's whining tone belied the gentle expression that came over his face as he cuddled the puppy. Jeremiah squirmed and squeaked as he nestled into the boy's lap. Irwin ran dirty fingertips over a ragged tear in the dog's skin. "Briars got him," he said.

"Yeah. Briars got him," Jonah repeated. He wiggled as close to Irwin as he could, imitating the older boy's stiff posture.

Mam smiled. "Looks like Jeremiah has made a new friend."

"Guess I could help, if you want," Irwin offered. "Take him out to do his business. Dogs like it outside."

"They do indeed," Ruth said. "I think you'll be good for Jeremiah."

"Me, too," Jonah joined in.

Ruth took a glass down from the cupboard and poured a tall glass of cold milk for Irwin and a tin cup, half full, for Jonah. She sliced a hardboiled egg onto a plate, added three fried chicken legs, two buttered biscuits, some cheese wedges and a handful of strawberries. She placed the food on a clean dish towel on an old three-legged milking stool beside the boys. "In case you need something to tide you over until supper."

Jonah nibbled at the cheese and ate a strawberry. Irwin swigged down the rest of the milk in less time than it took Ruth to spread her piecrust in a deep dish and fill it with sour cherries from last August's bounty. From the corner of her eye, Ruth saw Irwin dipping his index finger in the empty glass and letting Jeremiah suck drops of milk. Some of her uneasiness seeped away. Maybe there *was* hope for Irwin Beachy.

"We'll have a light meal tonight," Mam said. "We have that chicken-and-corn soup, chicken sandwiches and fresh salad. Stay for supper, Irwin."

He nodded. "Guess I could."

Anna went to the icebox and took out cold ham, applesauce and a plate of deviled eggs. "If we're having company, I think we'll need more than soup and sand-wiches, Mam."

Ruth and Miriam looked at each other. "A lot more," Ruth said, sending them both into fits of giggles. Even Susanna and the boys laughed, although it was clear they hadn't gotten the joke.

Ruth leaned on the counter and glanced around the kitchen at her family. This was where she belonged. This was where she was happiest. It was silly to think of ever leaving home or Mam and Susanna. This was where she was needed most, and it would be selfish to consider any-thing else, wouldn't it?

She sighed. Making hard choices was part of her faith. She had to do what was right, but how did she know what was right? Why did thoughts of Eli plague her so, and why did she remember every word he'd ever spoken to her? A small lump rose in her throat as she remembered how it had felt when he lifted her in his arms and carried her away from the burning schoolhouse. For an instant, she'd felt safe, safe in a way she hadn't since Dat had passed away.

But thinking of Eli in that way only made dandelion fluff tumble in the pit of her stomach. Moisture gathered in her eyes, and she blinked it away. Eli Lapp was not for her. He was trouble, and the less she had to do with him, the better. She was right; she knew she was right, so why did the clean male scent of him linger in the dark corners of her mind?

Saturday was a perfect spring day for the school picnic; the sun shone, and there was a slight breeze to keep every-one from getting overly warm. All of the parents and most of the relatives and friends who lived in the community turned out, as well as the young people's groups from two other churches.

Before picnic baskets were brought out, there was a volleyball game between the girls and boys. The bonnets won, hands down, because the bishop decreed that all the straw hats would have a handicap. The boys had their ankles tied together with lengths of corn string, so that they were hobbled. It made for many tumbles and even more laughter. After that came an egg and spoon race, adult men against their wives, and then men had been forced to use raw eggs. The losing team, consisting of fathers and grandfathers, would have to serve the children's lunch and clean up afterward.

Roman brought his red cart and driving goats, so that all the small children got rides. There was hymn singing by grades one through three, and a greased pig contest for boys between the ages of four and ten. After a hilarious contest and many near-misses, one of Lydia's children caught the pig and got to keep it, much to the delight of his mother.

"Roast suckling pig for Christmas dinner," she'd shouted. "Yum!" But everyone knew that they wouldn't really eat his pig. Samuel had promised to trade the greased pig, a male, for a young sow. The boy would use that pig to start his own breeding project. If he was diligent, he'd have the start of his own herd and be earning money from the animals by the time he was a teenager.

Throughout the afternoon, Ruth had stayed near Mam, helping to organize the games and prepare for the pie auction. She hadn't taken part in the volleyball because she didn't want to be anywhere near Eli. She'd taken enough teasing from her sisters about sitting in the porch swing with him, and she wasn't about to provide entertainment for the whole community.

Eli, thankfully, realized her reluctance to be seen talking to him and kept his distance, but that didn't keep him from watching her. Her cheeks burned from the intensity of his stare. No matter how busy she was, she couldn't ignore his scrutiny, and Miriam and Johanna had enjoyed every minute of her discomfort.

The day had gone well, but Ruth dreaded what was yet to come. As she'd suspected, her pie-making had been a disaster. She'd made a cherry pie, and when she'd put it in the oven, it had looked respectable. But the cherry filling had bubbled up, the crust had cracked down the middle and burned on the sides. Anna's pies were as perfect as the ones for sale behind the glass cases at Spence's Auction. Mam's pie was beautiful, Miriam's perfectly adequate. Hers was a disaster. And now everyone in the neighborhood would see what a terrible hand she was at baking, and she'd be teased for the next six months—maybe for the rest of her life.

Ruth had been tempted to stay up late and bake a half-dozen pies, hoping that at least one would turn out right, but she'd known better. With luck, no one would bid on her contribution and she could cut it into slices for the children's table. That way, she could discard the burned spots. Kids wouldn't care. They ate anything and didn't know the difference.

The problem was that every unmarried girl between the ages of fifteen and seventy had brought a pie and a picnic lunch that she would have to share with whichever man paid the most for her dessert. Of the older women, there was only Salome Byler and Gret Troyer, both widows and over sixty. Salome's pie was certain to be purchased by her brother Amos, out of pity and to see that no one was poisoned. He was used to her cooking. Salome had outlived three husbands, and Amos claimed that her pies had done in at least two of them. Gret was being courted by her third cousin, Jan Peachy, and Jan was sure to outbid anyone for her strawberry cream delight.

Everyone's eyes would be on her and Dorcas, both single, both old enough for people to whisper that it was time— high time—that they found a husband. Charley might give something for her pie, but Charley was such a tease. If he didn't like it, he'd let everyone know. And he would tease her worst of all. There were a couple of boys in Charley's gang, boys that she'd known all her life, some she even liked. But they'd not bid if Charley bid. And if he did or if he didn't, there was Eli. And who could guess what he would do?

Out of sheer cowardliness, Ruth hid her lunch basket and her pie under the table and covered them both with a spare tablecloth. Then she wandered away from the table, gathered up Johanna's baby girl and edged her way to the back of the crowd, near the buggies. Her stomach clenched and moisture dampened the hairs on the back of her neck. If only Mam and Samuel got so caught up in auctioning off the pies on the table that they'd forget all about hers. She could only hope luck was on her side.

Mam held Dorcas's raisin pie high over her head.

"What are we bid?" Samuel called in his deep auction-eer's voice. "Something in this lunch basket smells awfully good. Is that your mother's roast goose, Dorcas?"

"One dollar!" Charley shouted.

"None of that," Samuel flung back. "This is for the school, and we know your pockets are weighed down with greenbacks. We're starting this bidding at five dol-lars! Who'll say six?"

Six came and then seven. Amid good-natured catcalls and laughter, the price rose to nine dollars. Samuel brought the hammer down and handed Dorcas's lunch basket to a blushing boy from the north district. Dorcas took the pie, and the two went off amid whistles and hoots to find a place to spread their dinner cloth in the shade.

One after another, the pies went. They fairly flew off the table as money jingled and rustled into Mam's fire-fund tin oatmeal box. Amy's chocolate pie sold for twelve dollars, and then Charley bought Miriam's for fourteen dollars. Samuel claimed a frog in his throat, got the bishop to stand in for him as auctioneer and got a roar of approval when he successfully bid on both Anna's apple-cranberry pie and Mam's honey-pear, paying thirty dollars for the two of them.

"After all this shouting, I'm hungry enough to eat both lunches," Samuel bellowed. Everyone clapped. Last year, Anna's blackberry pie had brought only three dollars, and the boy that won the bid had been thirteen years old. Sharing lunch with her mother and her mother's beau and knowing hers was probably the tastiest pie of all might be a little disappointing to Anna, but she could take pleasure in knowing that she'd brought in so much for the school repairs.

One more pie went to one of Charley's buddies, and when the table was empty, Ruth thought she was home free. But then Mam whispered to Samuel, and he went back and pulled her pitiful cherry pie from its hiding place.

"Ruth Yoder made this one," Samuel said. "We all know what delicious pies those girls bake. Last chance here. Who's going to give me ten dollars for it?" He gave a quick glance at the pie and put it into the lunch basket.

"Fried chicken, coleslaw and potato salad," Johanna called. "Sweet pickles, corn bread and strawberries."

No one offered a bid.

"Ten dollars," Samuel said. "You won't regret it. I've eaten Ruth's fried chicken. And her corn bread is so light, you have to hold it down to eat it."

Nothing.

She'd hoped no one would buy her pie. But she hadn't

imagined how bad she would feel when there were no bids at all. Dorcas would never let her live it down.

"All right, you high rollers," Samuel said. "Nine dollars. Nine dollars for a pie you'd pay twelve for at Spence's."

"Ruth's was raw last year," Charley said. "How do we know what it tastes like?"

"As if you'd know," his mother chimed in. "You'd eat a dead horse if the buzzards didn't get to it first." That drew more laughter from the onlookers, but no offers for her pie.

Ruth wanted to crawl under the nearest buggy.

"Eight, eight. Who'll give me eight?"

"I will." Eli raised his hand. "But if I die of food poisoning, I'm blaming you, Samuel."

"Eight, eight. We have eight dollars from the young fellow from Belleville. Who'll give me nine?" Samuel chanted. "Nine dollars for fried chicken lunch and cherry pie."

"Might be burned cherry pie," Charley reminded them.

Snickers rippled through the audience.

"Going once," Samuel shouted. "Last chance, boys. I can taste that fried chicken." He lifted the lid on the lunch basket and peered inside. "Looks fine to me. Going twice. Any more takers?" He brought the hammer down with a bang. "Sold to Eli Lapp!"

Eli made his way through to the table and Samuel passed her lunch basket to him.

"Enjoy," Samuel said. "You got a real bargain." He glanced around. "Ruth! Where are you, Ruth? Pass that baby and come get your pie. This young buck has paid his money and wants his dinner."

Reluctantly, Ruth stepped forward.

Eli grinned.

Chapter Twelve

"I think there's a patch of shade under that old apple tree," Eli said as he took the picnic basket. "This feels heavy." He flashed a grin. "You brought lots of food. Good. I could eat a horse and chase the carriage."

"You might be better off with the horse," she answered. Her cheeks were burning. People were laughing and watching her. Even Susanna was giggling. "I'm not the best pie baker."

"I'll be the judge of that. It's cherry, isn't it?"

"Cherry crisp, more like it," she replied. She followed him, keeping her eyes on his back, trying not to make eye contact with her neighbors. Soon everyone would see just how pitiful a pie Eli had spent his money on. Then they'd all start talking about how it was just as well that she didn't want to marry, because who would want a wife who couldn't make a simple cherry pie?

Families and couples everywhere were spreading cloths to share their lunches. Samuel's twin sons were racing around Mam's basket, and his younger daughter Lori Ann had a thumb in her mouth and was hiding behind his legs. She was a shy little thing who stuttered and suffered from the loss of her mother. Maybe the neighbors were right about it being time for Samuel to put off his mourning and remarry. But why did he have to choose Mam?

Ruth couldn't see her mother accepting Samuel as the new head of the household. It was right that the husband and father assume that place, but Mam had her own way of doing things. They were making out so well that Ruth couldn't imagine Mam or the rest of them adjusting to a new husband's and stepfather's ways. Home wouldn't feel the same.

"How's this?" Eli's question tugged her back into the moment.

"Oh, fine." She would have preferred sitting in the apple orchard alone with Eli, just to escape the stares, but that wasn't an option. She dreaded opening the picnic basket. Everyone would see her poor excuse for a pie and the teasing would start all over again. They'd poke fun at her and at Eli for buying it. She didn't know why she'd let Anna pack it. They should have left it at home or thrown it to the chickens. "I still think you wasted your money," she ventured. "Even if it was a donation for repairing the school."

Eli waited expectantly for her to take out the tablecloth and spread it on the ground. Everyone else was already eating, and if they were too slow, they'd miss the children's sack races later.

"Let's see Ruth's pie!" Charley called from where he sat on a blanket beside Miriam, only a few feet away. He was already halfway through one of her ham sandwiches. "If it's too tough, you can always use the crust for a wagon wheel."

Eli threw him a look that could have scorched paper.

Ruth kneeled on the tablecloth, shut her eyes and lifted the lid. *What a coward I am,* she thought as she fumbled for the pie. She didn't want to see how ridiculous the burned crust looked, compared to all the pretty pies.

"Careful," Eli warned. "You wouldn't want to drop it."

She glanced down. She had the pie firmly in her hands, but it was all she could do not to gasp for air like a landed fish. *This wasn't her pie!*

This crust was full and golden brown, rising high and dimpled with a pattern of cherries cut into the top, each cut just wide enough to allow the rich red filling inside to bubble up. The edges around the pie were neatly scored, not burned, but perfect and appealing. Ruth could never, in a million years, have made such a beautiful pie.

In an instant, she realized that Anna must have substituted Ruth's ruined pie with one of her own before they left the house. She didn't know when her sister had done it, but it was clear that she had. Had Anna really thought anyone would believe Ruth had made this? But the look on Eli's face answered her question. He was smiling with admiration—at the pie *and* Ruth.

She placed the picture-perfect pie in the center of the checkered tablecloth before glancing across the school yard to see if Anna and her mother were watching. They were talking with Samuel's children, paying her no attention. Now what? Did Ruth just blurt out the truth? It would be dishonest to pretend that she'd baked the pie when she hadn't, but if she came clean now, Charley would make her the butt of his jokes at every gathering for years.

As if thinking about him had drawn him closer, Charley gave a sharp whistle. She looked up to see him standing over her picnic basket. "Would you look at that?" he said, making a show of rubbing his eyes. "Ruth's pie isn't burned this year."

Around her, heads were turning. Dorcas's lunch partner stretched his neck to stare at them.

"You'll be burned if you don't get back here and eat

Courting Ruth

my pie," Miriam said, loud enough for those around her to hear.

Everyone laughed, turning the joke on Charley as he hurried back to his own picnic lunch.

Ruth began removing the sugared peaches and potato salad from the picnic basket, still in a dilemma as to what to say. "Charley's okay," she answered. "He just likes to tease. Isn't he a cousin of yours? Your mother was a Byler, wasn't she?"

"If Charley's a cousin, he must be a fourth or fifth cousin. Not close enough to count. Not when he still has his eye on this pie."

Ruth met his gaze and they both chuckled. Suddenly she felt shy, and she busied herself preparing the feast. He sat, stretching long legs out while she still knelt. "You didn't have to buy my lunch, you know," she said. She'd tell him about the pie when no one was watching them. She unfolded foil-wrapped chicken and passed Eli a plate and several paper napkins.

"Looks like I got the bargain here and the prettiest girl to share my lunch with." He sprinkled salt and pepper on a chicken leg and looked up at her. "No need to get all red-cheeked and flustered. It's just eating on the ground. We're not breaking any rules."

"*Ne,* we are not." In spite of her fears, she was having a good time with Eli. He didn't seem like a flirt or a fast boy today. He felt like someone she'd always known, someone she could be comfortable spending the afternoon with whether it was having a picnic lunch or working on the farm. Still, what she was doing—taking credit for her sister's baking—wasn't honest. She should explain to him what had happened this instant. She started to say something, but Eli spoke first.

"This is nice, being here with you. I'm glad I came,

Ruth. And I wouldn't have let anybody else win that bid if I'd had to go to thirty dollars."

"Thirty dollars? That would be too much," she protested, but tingles of delight ran up her spine to think that he would do such a thing for her.

"Why not? I earn my wages with my own two hands, the same as anyone else here. I have no one to support. Why shouldn't I spend what I like to support the school? And you," he added. "Mostly you."

Ruth bit off a small piece of chicken and chewed, but she didn't taste it. Eli made her feel the way she had felt the day years ago when she'd climbed Aunt Martha's big oak tree on a dare. From the top branch, she'd been able to see the farms all around. She was so high that the cows had looked as small as geese. She'd been so dizzy-headed that she'd been both thrilled and afraid. She had stayed there for an hour, too scared to climb down. Yet it gave her a thrill whenever she remembered it. Sitting here with Eli as her date was like that. Just looking at him made her giddy. More than that, Eli didn't talk nonstop like Charley. Eli didn't mind letting her just catch her breath and enjoy the sunshine and the day.

She glanced across the school yard at her mother. Irwin was standing beside Mam. Ruth couldn't hear what they were saying, but Anna handed him a plate of food, and the boy sat down in the grass beside Mam's spread.

Maybe her mother was right about the boy, Ruth thought. Perhaps he was lonely and misunderstood. But as she watched, the minute Mam walked away, Irwin stuck out a foot and tripped ten-year-old Rudy. He fell on his face, smashing his muffin, and Irwin laughed.

Ruth was about to get up when Mam started to give Irwin what for. She didn't need to raise her voice. When Mam was angry, her eyes said it all. A few words from her were worse than any spanking Ruth had ever gotten from Dat.

"Ruth? Are you listening to me?" Eli asked.

She glanced at him. "Irwin just—"

"Samuel and your mother can handle Irwin."

He was right. "I'm sorry. What were you saying?"

Eli's expression was serious. "I want to talk to you about us. You can't pretend that what happened in the movies or the orchard or your porch swing wasn't real."

She looked down at her chicken leg, all too aware of how deeply she'd allowed herself to feel for him.

"I've never felt this way about a girl before," he continued. "And I think you like me."

She sighed and laid the chicken on her napkin. Suddenly, explaining about the pie switch didn't seem all that important. "I *do* like you. It's just more complicated than you make it. Liking you isn't enough."

"Was it wrong of me to come here today? Don't you want me here?"

She looked into his blue eyes. "I do want you here, Eli, but even more, I want you at church tomorrow. Don't disappoint Mam."

"Your mother or you?"

"Both of us," she admitted. Hope rose in her chest and she tried not to let it envelop her. Thinking about Eli… about her and Eli and the future was too much. There were too many obstacles, too much that she was unsure of. She didn't know what she wanted, what God wanted, and what had happened with Eli and that girl.

"I'll try not to. But for today, let's just enjoy the picnic and have fun. Please?"

"All right," she agreed, taking one last look at the pie. She wouldn't ruin the day. She'd make it right tomorrow. She'd tell him she hadn't baked the pie. And if Eli came to services, that might change everything. No matter what he'd done wrong back home, if he was truly repentant, he could find forgiveness, couldn't he? That was the beauty of the faith. God could forgive anything.

Eli held out his plate. "Could I have another chicken leg and some of that potato salad? And maybe some strawberries?"

She laughed and removed two more bowls from the bottom of the basket. "Wait until you see what else is in here," she said. "You might not want to fill up on sweets yet."

"I don't know. My mam always said I had a liking for sweet things."

Ruth blushed, certain he wasn't talking about sliced strawberries.

Early Monday morning, as soon as the kitchen was readied up, the dishes washed and dried and put away and the floors swept, Ruth hurried out to the garden to pick peas and hoe around the kale, spinach and radishes. Miriam would need her after lunch to help in the fields, but if she hurried, she'd have time to run an important errand.

She needed to go to the chair shop and explain to Eli about the pie. She had asked Anna after breakfast why she hadn't warned her that she exchanged pies, but Anna had only laughed and gone back to skimming cream off a pan of milk and humming the tune from an old hymn. Nothing she said could convince Anna to talk about baking or pies or auctions. Anna was easygoing, but she could be the most stubborn one of all of them.

Eli had kept his word and come to church the day before, but they'd had no time to speak in private. During services, Eli had sat on the men's side of the room, while she had sat with the women. And since the worship was held at their

home, she and Mam and her sisters had been extra busy
with serving food and welcoming visitors.

The weather had been so good that the young people
had set up long tables in the yard, and the communal meal
had been held there. Men ate at the first sitting, and there
had barely been time to grab a bite herself and help with
the children before the second sermon.

The only contact she'd had with Eli had been when she'd
handed him a plate of corn bread and filled his glass with
cold milk. But that hadn't meant that she was unaware of
him. He had been watching her all day, and it had made
her self-conscious and fearful that she'd drop a bowl of
peas and dumplings on the visiting bishop from Ohio or
trip and fall facedown into Aunt Martha's shoofly pie.

After church, there had been visiting and cleanup. Ruth
had seen Eli folding tables and chairs and putting them in
the special wagon, and she'd seen him helping with the
buggies, but all too soon, the day of worship had been
over. The family had gone to bed early, tired, but full of
peace…all but her. She'd tossed and turned, determined
that she had to get the matter of the pie straightened out.
Like untangling a knotted ball of yarn, she had to start
with one end and work her way through her problems. If
she told the truth and cleared her conscience, she might
be in a better place to solve the bigger issue of what to do
about Eli.

Eli rubbed his fingertips along a chair leg, feeling for
rough spots. When he found one, he carefully sanded the
maple with the finest grade of sandpaper until the wood
was as smooth as glass. He and Roman had been working
in the shop since breakfast. Roman had been gluing chair
backs and seats together and applying strapping so that they

would dry properly, until Aunt Fannie had appeared in the doorway that led to the display area and called to him.

Eli could tell that his aunt had been out of sorts at breakfast this morning, not angry but worried about something. The way she'd glanced at him out of the corner of her eye made him suspect her fuss had to do with him, but he couldn't think of anything he'd done to upset her. Both his aunt and his uncle had seemed pleased that he'd gone to the school picnic and to church with them on Sunday, although neither had commented on it.

Spiritual matters were generally considered too private to discuss, even between family members. If and when he joined the Old Amish Church, it would be his decision, and no matter how much his aunt and uncle might want him to accept the faith, that was between him and God.

Now he couldn't help overhearing as Aunt Fannie said, "This came on Saturday. I thought you should see it first."

His uncle answered her, but his voice was too soft for Eli to hear what he said. Eli knew that it was wrong to eavesdrop, but he was curious. And the only way to avoid hearing would be to put down his work and leave the shop. Then he'd be forced to explain why he'd walked away from a task. Whatever it was that had upset his aunt, it wasn't good. If he'd caused a problem for Roman, he wanted to straighten it out.

"*Ne,* it's your house," Aunt Fannie protested.

"It's addressed to Eli. Give it to him."

"Look at it! That's her name, isn't it?"

Eli dropped the sandpaper and stood up, the chair leg still in his hand. He walked toward the front room, but stopped when his uncle walked back into the shop.

"Mail for you." Roman held out a letter. "Fannie should

have given it to you Saturday when you got home from the picnic."

Eli took the envelope. In the left corner, a name was printed clearly in blue ink. Hazel had written to him, and the return address was a town in Virginia. Shocked, he looked up at Roman.

The older man's face was creased with concern, but his gaze held no judgment. "It was wrong of Fannie to keep your mail from you. You'll want to read it in private. The work can wait a few minutes."

Eli nodded. He took the letter outside into the backyard and sat down on a bale of straw. His heart was beating fast. He hadn't thought he'd hear from Hazel. He'd worried about her and wondered how she was, but he hadn't expected this—not after the way they'd parted.

He turned the envelope over in his hand. It couldn't have weighed more than half an ounce, but it felt as heavy as if it were made of cement. Guilt settled over him, and the events of that night at the bonfire came rushing back to haunt him. Catching his lower lip between his teeth, he slowly opened the letter.

There was a page and a half, printed from a computer. Only the signature was handwritten. He read through it twice and sat there for a while trying to decide what to do. He closed his eyes. The sun was warm on his face, and the air smelled of green growing things. From the yard, he heard the bleat of a goat and the flapping sound of clothes drying on a line. Yesterday, when he was listening to the hymns, he'd felt a peace inside. Now he searched for that quiet peace.

After a quarter of an hour, he rose and went to find Roman.

His uncle had returned to strapping the chair parts so

that the glue would dry properly. Eli held out the folded pages of the letter.

"Why should I read that?" Roman concentrated on the buckle he was tightening. "It is your business."

"Aunt Fannie is right. I live in your house, and I'm part of your family. You should know what it says. Please." Eli held it out for him and this time Roman took it.

Eli's uncle went to the bench for his spectacles, blew the sawdust off them, and then wiped them on his blue cotton shirt. He read the letter slowly. When he had finished, he nodded, and handed the letter back. "I see," he said. "And what will you do about this?"

"I don't know. Think about it, I guess."

"And pray," Roman advised. "It's always best."

Eli was cleaning up his work space when Ruth entered by the back door. He turned and surprise showed on his face. He smiled. "Ruth."

"Eli." She glanced around, hoping Roman wasn't here. As she'd walked down the road, she'd thought about what she would say, of just how she would explain the confusion about the pie. Now that she was here with him, she felt just as tongue-tied as ever. Her palms felt damp, and it seemed stuffy in the shop. "I need to talk to you. In private."

"Something I've done wrong?"

She shook her head. "*Ne.* Something I've done wrong."

"Okay." He led her back outside, around the corner of the shop to Fannie's grape arbor. There was a wooden bench there, and he waved her to the seat.

"I'd just as soon stand," she said, feeling more anxious by the moment. She just wanted to get this over with.

He hooked his thumbs into his thin red suspenders and stood arms akimbo, waiting.

Heat flashed under her skin. She stared down at her new black sneakers. She'd been ashamed to walk down the road in bare feet, for fear some English would see her and make fun, but now she felt that that might have been *Hochmut*—that she might have worn the new shoes to show off for Eli. She twisted her hands in her apron. "I wanted to…"

"What is it, Ruth?"

"The pie," she blurted. "It wasn't mine. I didn't bake it. It was Anna's."

He laughed. "Whoever made it, it was good."

She looked up at him. "*Ne,* you don't understand. I let everyone think that it was mine. I took credit for my sister's baking. I deceived—"

"Wicked," he agreed, but he was still shaking with amusement.

"This is serious. Stop laughing at me." She crossed her arms over her chest.

"Do you think I care who made the pie?"

"You should. You paid for it. And if you'd gotten mine—the one I made, you would—"

"Wait. Let me get this straight." He dropped onto the high-backed bench and motioned for her to sit beside him. When she didn't immediately do so, he rolled his eyes. "Sit," he commanded.

Ruth exhaled softly and obeyed, taking care to keep a distance between them. "I didn't mean to take credit for Anna's baking. I made my own pie, but I think Anna switched it."

"So…it wasn't your fault? You didn't know?"

"I knew after we opened the basket. When I saw it. But I didn't say anything. I let you go on believing that it was mine." She lowered her gaze. "I think a part of me wanted you to think I could bake a pie that pretty."

"So now you've come to straighten it all out?"

She nodded.

He turned toward her and caught her hands in his. "All right, you've told me. Your conscience should be clear. Why didn't you tell me right away?"

"I don't know. I was already embarrassed by all the attention. I didn't want Charley to find out. He would have made everything worse."

"And this has worried you since the picnic?"

"I couldn't sleep," she confessed. "I'm an awful pie baker. But I'm an honest person."

"The most honest I've ever known," he said. She tried to pull out of his grasp, but his big hands held hers tightly.

"Don't make fun of me. What I did was wrong."

"Are you sorry?"

"Of course, I am." She looked at him. "Why would I come here to tell you, if I wasn't sorry?"

"And you won't do it again?"

"Never!"

"Then it's over, Ruth. You've nothing more to be ashamed of."

"I don't want you to think bad of me."

"I could never do that." He slid closer to her. "There's something—"

"Ruth!"

Ruth's heart sank as her mother came around the end of the grape arbor.

"What goes on here?" Mam folded her arms over her chest and glared at them. "The two of you have some explaining to do."

Chapter Thirteen

"It's not what you think," Eli said, letting go of Ruth's hand and getting to his feet.

Mam glared at him. "You don't know what I think. My daughters aren't fast girls. You may do things differently in Belleville, but here holding hands is for couples who have publicly stated their intention to marry."

"We weren't…" Ruth began.

"I have eyes to see," Mam said. "Being alone together like this is unseemly." She paused and continued in a softer voice. "You know that there is already talk about you, Eli. It's not fair to Ruth for you to endanger her reputation."

Ruth heard Eli's temper flare. "We weren't doing anything wrong."

Mam looked back toward the shop. "Samuel's buggy is in front. It's best if you come with me, Ruth."

"It's the middle of a school day. Why are you even here?" Ruth demanded. Eli was right. They hadn't done anything wrong. Why did her mother have to assume the worst? And how had she known where to find them? Why was she looking? "Did Anna tell you I was coming to the shop?"

"You mean, am I spying on you?"

Mam's hazel eyes took on the glint of polished pewter, and Ruth's heart sank.

"Why would you think such a thing?" Mam's tone barely masked her hurt feelings. "When have I *ever* spied on you?"

"It's my fault," Eli said. "Don't blame Ruth. There was a misunderstanding and we were talking and…"

Mam silenced him with a raised palm. "Eli, please. It's best if Ruth and I discuss this in private."

"Mam!" she protested. "Don't make more of this than—"

"The children are on their noon break," her mother cut in. "Elmer has an abscessed tooth, and Lydia asked me to call our dentist. I borrowed Samuel's horse and buggy to save time coming to use the phone." Lines at the corners of her eyes deepened. "I didn't know you were here until I arrived and Fannie told me where to find you, thinking I knew you were here."

Eli frowned and gestured. "Great. Now here comes Roman."

Ruth heard the scrape of gravel and turned to see the older man striding down the path, followed by his two yapping rat terriers. She glanced back at Eli and said softly, "I'd best go."

He nodded. "We'll talk later."

"Eli?" Roman brushed sawdust off his worn leather apron as he approached. "Is there something?" He looked from Eli to Mam as the yipping little dogs darted past him. "Quiet!" he ordered. The brown and white terriers leaped up, stub tails wagging. "Get down, I say. Behave." His cheeks reddened. "Fannie spoils them."

"The dogs are fine." Mam leaned to pet one and then the other. "No treats today," she told the terriers.

"I thought there might be…" Roman tugged at his beard and glanced at Eli "…a problem here."

"Mam came to use the phone," Ruth explained. "I'm riding back to the school with her." She averted her gaze as she hurried past Roman. It was bad enough that Mam had embarrassed her in front of Eli. She didn't want to drag his aunt and uncle into it.

As she walked to the buggy behind her mother, feeling like a chastised child, she felt Eli's gaze on her back. She wanted to turn back, to try to make things right with him, but she didn't. Maybe because she was afraid, afraid of what she might say. What she might not ever be able to say.

The two women disappeared around the side of the chair shop. For a moment, Roman and Eli looked at each other without speaking, and then Eli said, "We were talking and Hannah came along. She didn't think us sitting alone here looked proper. But we needed to talk." He scuffed the ground with his boot. "You know, about things."

One of the terriers nipped playfully at the hem of Roman's black pants, and he shook it off. "Did you tell her about the letter?"

Eli worked his jaw but didn't respond.

"It's right that they should know."

"Hazel wrote to me. It's not a matter to be gossiped about."

"*Ne,* but you need to tell Ruth. If you're familiar enough with each other to sit on the bench alone together, you're familiar enough that she needs to know." He paused. "And around here, what concerns one of us, concerns all." Roman slipped his thumbs under his black suspenders. "Fannie's worked herself up pretty well over it. That letter."

"Did you tell her what Hazel said?" Eli's gaze searched his uncle's face.

"Not my place." Roman was quiet again for a moment and then went on. "If you've a mind to settle here—and you know you're welcome in our home—you need to make peace with your mother. It's the only way to make things right…to think about starting your own family."

Eli understood what he was talking about. If he had any thoughts whatsoever of making a home and a life with Ruth, he needed to tell her what had happened with Hazel. But why should he have to? Why couldn't Ruth take him for the person he was today? Not back then, back there.

"Then there's the matter of the church," Roman said.

Eli tightened his fingers into fists at his sides. "You mean I'd have to join if I want any chance with Ruth."

"It's your choice, joining the church or not. You have to decide for yourself what you want from this world," he said, obviously feeling awkward. "But I wouldn't be telling the truth if I didn't tell you it's what I wish for you…what I've prayed for."

Eli was surprised that his uncle would say these personal things to him. This wasn't the kind of thing Plain people talked about, especially men, and he knew it had to be difficult for his uncle. But Roman had always been a little different. His grandfather had called him weak, but he wasn't. Eli wished he had the inner strength Roman possessed.

"I think you'd find peace," Roman added.

"You don't know how I've struggled over it. I don't know what to do." Eli couldn't look Roman in the eyes any longer. "I'm not certain if I belong in the church or in the outside world. I'm not certain where I belong."

"Hard to know when you've been uprooted the way you were. Kind of like seedlings that have been transplanted.

They get confused sometimes, growing one direction, then the other." Roman looked off in the distance. A blue jay cackled. "Your *grand* was a hard man, not just on you, but on himself. I always thought your mother should have kept you at home with her. You'd have gotten used to a stepfather. Joseph would have been fair with you."

Eli shrugged. "Maybe it was best they sent me away. They say I'm like my dat. Maybe I'm his son, more than hers. Headed for a bad end."

Roman grimaced. "I've heard that said, but I don't believe it. I knew your father, Eli. There was a lot of good in him. If he'd lived, I think he would have come back to us...to his family and his faith."

A lump rose in Eli's throat, and he didn't answer, afraid his voice would crack. He wasn't exactly embarrassed by his emotion, but it wasn't something one man shared with another.

"You hear what I'm saying?" Roman's own voice filled with feeling, surprising Eli. "*I knew him.* And I don't see the bad side of him in you." He looked in the direction the two women had gone. "Just be sure you don't take a path that's not yours. And don't take along somebody else with you. You're better than that."

Eli knew he was talking about Ruth. "I care about her. A lot. I'd do nothing to hurt her."

Roman walked away, the dogs trailing him. "Then see you don't."

"Why did you have to say anything about marriage?" Ruth agonized aloud when she and her mother were alone in the buggy. She sat up straight and gripped the leathers in both hands as a pickup truck pulling a boat whizzed past them on the road. "And why did you mention the gossip about him? It's not like you to be uncharitable."

"And it's unlike you to be caught holding hands with a boy in Fannie's grape arbor," Mam returned. "Fannie saw the two of you. What must she think?"

No other traffic was in sight, and Ruth used the break to cross the intersection onto the quieter road that led to the school.

Mam's chin went up, and she planted both black leather shoes together on the floorboard. "There's something you need to know for your own good. Eli had a letter from the girl."

Ruth's stomach turned over. She didn't know what to say.

"You know who I mean," her mother continued. "The girl who accused him."

"A letter from her doesn't mean that Eli's guilty of anything wrong." But it *could* mean that they still cared for each other, Ruth thought. Or it could mean she was trying to start trouble for him again. Now, here in Seven Poplars. "I suppose Fannie told you about the letter."

"She did but not to hurt Eli or you. She wanted to protect you, to keep you from being harmed."

"Fannie's his aunt. She's supposed to—"

"She thought I should know and that you should know. Fannie is a sweet woman. She'd never intentionally spread rumors and the letter wasn't a rumor. It was real. She held it in her hands and read Hazel's name on the envelope before turning it over to Roman, who gave it to Eli."

Moisture clouded Ruth's eyes, but she kept her gaze on the horse and the road ahead. "Do you know what happened to her? The girl? Her church didn't shun her, did they?"

"*Ne,* but Martha says the girl ran away after the baby was born. No one knows where she is. Except Eli, maybe," she added.

"She ran away with an infant?" Compassion flooded Ruth's heart. "I can't imagine. Her family must be so worried."

"She didn't take the baby, an older sister did. The sister and her husband live out west somewhere. They'd been married six years without being blessed with children. Martha said that it was Hazel's idea to let them adopt the infant. The girl said she wasn't ready to be a mother."

Ruth had no answer for that. She couldn't imagine giving birth to a child and not raising it. But considering the circumstances, perhaps the girl's decision had been the right one. No one among the Plain people would hold a baby responsible for the mother's mistake.

"So you see why Fannie thought you should know he'd heard from her." Mam's voice was gentle this time.

But Ruth didn't want soft words. She felt all in turmoil inside: scared, angry. "Eli isn't the type of boy who would get a girl in trouble and not marry her!"

"Ruth, Ruth, Ruth, what's come over you?" Her mother stared at her, obviously not approving of her passionate outburst.

"Nothing. I simply refuse to believe such a thing about Eli."

"So you *do* like him."

"As a friend."

"Sounds to me like *more* than a friend," her mother said, shaking her head. "Daughter, I'm worried about you. You're like an apron on the clothesline, flapping in the wind, one way and then the other."

Ruth pulled hard on the right rein, guiding the gelding off the road and onto the grass shoulder before yanking the horse to a halt. The dapple gray stopped so quickly that the buggy swayed. "What's that supposed to mean?"

"It means that until Eli Lapp came to Seven Poplars,

you knew your own mind. You said you knew what you wanted. You told me that you weren't going to marry, that you would remain at home with me and Susanna. The past two weeks, you've lollygagged in the orchard with the boy, sat on the porch swing in the dark with him, and the two of you have been caught holding hands in the grape arbor." She gestured outward with her hand. "Not to mention going to the movie or eating together at the school picnic. You say you're not courting, but it looks like it to me."

Ruth didn't know what to say. How could she explain to Mam that she hadn't intended to do any of those things with Eli? They'd just happened. How could she tell her how giddy he made her feel inside? She swallowed. "I don't believe Eli would ever abandon his child. There must be more to the story."

"Have you asked him?" Mam was angry. She never shouted like Aunt Martha, but the angrier she became, the lower her tone of voice.

Ruth slapped the reins over the horse's back, and the buggy lurched forward. "I wouldn't pry." She glanced at her mother. "Aren't you always telling us not to judge?"

"*Ya*, that I do say. So the Bible tells us. But it also speaks about children respecting their parents."

Ruth nibbled at her lower lip as the horse broke into a trot. "Have I been disrespectful?"

"You just accused me of being uncharitable."

"I didn't mean it, not really. I'm sorry."

Hannah sighed, sitting back on the buggy seat. "You have always been a good daughter, one your father would be proud of. But the time has come for you to make up your mind about what you want and follow that path. You need to think before you act. You need to set a good example for your sisters and the younger girls in the community."

The horse's hooves clicked rhythmically against the

road. "We really weren't doing anything wrong in the grape arbor," Ruth said.

"An action doesn't have to be wrong to give the appearance of mischief. What if it hadn't been me who found the two of you, but your uncle Reuben or aunt Martha? Because we're women alone, we have to guard our reputations even more than if your father was alive. Especially since I teach at the school."

"You're right. I didn't think." Shame flooded through Ruth. If people complained, they might think that Mam was at fault for not teaching her daughters proper behavior. The school board could decide not to renew her contract next year. "What do you want me to do, Mam?"

"I don't want you to do something you'll regret for the rest of your life."

"That doesn't answer my question."

"*Ya,* but what I want is not important. You're old enough to make up your own mind what your life will be. You must decide. You aren't like Miriam. You've joined the church."

"I feel awful, Mam. We never argue. I don't want to upset you."

"And I don't mean to be harsh with you, but it's time you act like a grown woman."

There was silence for a moment, except for the clippity-clop of the horse's hooves, before Hannah spoke again. "Look into your heart, daughter. Your path will become clear."

"I want to do what God wants," Ruth said.

"You have only to listen. He will tell you." She pulled a pocket watch from her apron and her expression softened. "Lunch break should be over." She took a black lunch box from under the seat, opened it, retrieving a sandwich.

"Have half of this," she offered. "It's your favorite, chicken salad."

Ruth took her section of the sandwich, heading up the lane to the school. "I haven't heard the bell yet," she said between bites.

Mam folded the waxed paper and put it back in the lunch box to use again tomorrow. "I left Elvie in charge of the little ones," she explained. "She might be so busy making eyes at Elmer over her lunch that she didn't notice the time."

Ruth couldn't help smiling. "Elvie and Elmer? She's too young to be thinking of boyfriends yet, isn't she?"

"Elmer is more interested in Eli's motorbike than girls, but Elvie has always liked him, and he could do worse. Her parents are good church members and solid, God-fearing people. Besides, Elvie is the oldest, and she has no brothers. She'll inherit land."

"Don't tell me you're matchmaking your eighth graders."

Mam laughed. "Not me. But Elvie knows her own mind. Mark my words, when he turns eighteen, Elmer will be trailing after Elvie like a fly on jam. And we'll be going to a wedding."

By the time they reached the school yard, Ruth had acknowledged to herself the truth of her indecision. She *had* been vacillating, whipping in the wind, not knowing what direction she was going. It was just that Eli had confused her. The way he made her feel when he was close confused her. He made her doubt her decision to remain unmarried.

But it was clear what Mam thought and wanted. Ruth would pray, but obviously her duty was to her family. Mam was no longer a young woman. She'd reached her mid-forties, and she needed the care and devotion of a daughter.

It would never work out with Eli, anyway, Ruth told herself. He was too handsome for her, too good a catch to really be interested in her. He didn't really want to court her. He was just pursuing her because she'd told him she wasn't interested.

Ruth needed to just let the whole thing go. She wasn't meant to be a wife. And in time, her deep attraction to Eli would pass. The happiness and well-being of those she loved most must come ahead of any personal desires.

It seemed like the right thing to do, but Ruth's heart felt heavy. Never to marry… It would be a sacrifice, maybe a greater one than she'd ever expected, since Eli came into her life. The heaviness in her chest turned to an ache in the pit of her stomach and spread through her. Resolutely, she pushed back the image of Eli's face and the sound of his voice. She would be strong…she would do what was right…what God wanted.

As she reined the horse into the drive that led alongside the school, Ruth saw that Mam had been right. The students were still at recess that followed lunch, some playing ball, others on the swings, and a few still finishing their lunches. Lydia's Abraham, a gangly nine-year-old, was walking the top rail of the split-rail fence with his lunch bucket balanced on top of his head. Elvie, who was supposed to be in charge, was nowhere in sight.

"See, what did I tell you?" Mam said. "Recess should have been over ten minutes ago."

Eleven-year-old Herman came running around the school, saw the buggy and shouted, "Teacher's back!" As children hurried toward the building from all directions, Abraham lost his footing and tumbled off the fence. The boy rolled and came up on his feet laughing, none the worse for wear. One of his brothers had reached the steps and was ringing the cast-iron bell to signal the start of classes.

Mam got out of the buggy. "I don't see Samuel," she said. "He must have walked home. Can you take the rig back to his barn?"

Ruth nodded. "I'm sorry about what happened."

"Let it be for now. But think on what I said. You have decisions to make."

"I think I already have, Mam. Don't worry. I'd never do anything to shame you or my sisters, I promise."

The entrance to Samuel's lane was only a few hundred yards south of the schoolhouse. Once Mam had her lunch box and notebook, Ruth guided the horse in a circle, preparing to drive out of the yard. But as she turned right, she noticed two boys wrestling on the ground next to the shed. "Hey, you two," she called. "Recess is over. Didn't you hear the bell?"

Irwin scrambled to his feet, grabbed his hat off the grass and shoved something into his pocket. The top button was missing off his shirt, and one suspender hung off his shoulder. Weeds were tangled in his scarecrow hair. The other boy, Samuel's son Peter, had more guilt than dirt on his face, and his shirttail was out, but he seemed to have gotten the best of the tussle.

"Were you two fighting?" Ruth demanded. She got down out of the buggy and walked toward them. "Irwin, what did you put in your pocket?"

Peter's face blushed a deep red, and he looked as though he were about to burst into tears.

Irwin hung his head and stared at his bare feet.

"Well, Irwin, I'm waiting."

"What's wrong?" Mam came up behind her. "Why are you boys out here when everyone else has gone inside?"

"I think they were fighting." Ruth dropped her hands to

her hips. "Irwin put something in his pocket, and he won't show me what it is."

"Were you fighting?" her mother asked.

A tear rolled down Peter's cheek. *"Ya,"* he squeaked. "We was."

"I'm ashamed of you both." Ruth looked from one boy to the other. "Peter, what would your father say?"

"There is a better way to solve problems than violence." He mimicked Samuel's deep baritone voice so well that it was all Ruth could do not to smile.

"Your father is right," Mam said. "Fighting is not our way. You both are old enough to know better." She held out her hand. "Irwin? What do you have?"

He took a step backward and reluctantly dug into his pocket and produced a pack of matches.

"Is this what you were fighting over?"

More tears streaked Peter's face as he nodded.

"Are these yours, Irwin?" Mam took them from him.

He didn't answer.

"Peter, do you have anything you want to say about this?"

The boy shook his head.

"Very well. Peter, you take your father's horse and buggy home and come right back. Tell him that you will be staying after school today. You will both write, *'There is a better way to solve problems than violence,'* two hundred times in your best cursive. And you will both stay after tomorrow afternoon to scrub the schoolhouse floor, wash the blackboards and the windows. Is that clear?"

"Ya," Peter said.

Irwin nodded.

"I will keep the matches." Mam tucked them into her apron. "If I ever catch either of you with matches again, you *and* your father, Peter—and in your case Irwin, Lydia and

Norman—will answer to the school board. Now, off with you. Irwin, I hope you remembered your math homework today."

Both boys ran.

Ruth watched the boys go. "Something has to be done about Irwin before someone is seriously hurt."

"Something has to be done all right, but I have a feeling there's more to this than they're telling. You see the look in Peter's eyes? You, of all people, Ruth, know things aren't always what they appear. I'll get to the bottom of this, I promise you."

"I just hope it's not too late. He's on our farm all the time. What if he burns our house down?"

"He isn't going to burn the house down or hurt any of us. He's an unhappy child, and we have to find a way to help him."

"He's a bully. You saw him trip Rudy at the picnic. He's always shoving or—" Ruth sighed in exasperation. "Mam, you're too easy on him. He's a real troublemaker. And he seems to have it out for Samuel's twins. He picks on them the most."

"And why is that, do you suppose?"

Ruth stared at her mother.

"What do Rudy and Peter have that Irwin doesn't?"

"A father, but—"

"A father who adores them." Hannah started across the grass toward the schoolhouse, and Ruth walked with her. "Their own ponies. New shoes and new lunch buckets."

"But Lydia and Norman are good to him. It's Irwin that makes people dislike him," Ruth said.

"He has a good heart, daughter. And if we can find a way to reach it, Irwin will return the love we give him twofold."

"I think you've already given him too many chances."

"Doesn't the Lord do that with us? No matter how many times we fail Him, His love is always there for us. We must try to do as much for Irwin, Ruth. If we can't give him hope and a sense of belonging, he will be as lost to us as his family is to him. And that I couldn't bear, as a teacher or as a mother."

Chapter Fourteen

Morning sales at Spence's were so busy that it was one o'clock by the time Ruth felt she could leave Miriam. She'd made plans to have lunch at the Amish Market with Dorcas and two of their girlfriends, and the girls were waiting impatiently to go. Charley's sister Mary and her cousin Jane had already sold all their cut flowers and herbs and packed their wagon for the trip home.

"Go on." Miriam waved them away. "I'll be fine. John said he'd bring me back a sandwich and lemonade."

Jane whispered something to her cousin, and the two giggled.

"I see how it is," Mary teased. "Miriam wants to get rid of us so she can talk to the cute new vet."

"Dr. Hartman is a friend of the family," Miriam corrected, but Ruth noticed how merrily her sister's eyes twinkled. Mam had called John, who had recently joined his grandfather's large animal practice, to help deliver a calf that spring, and he and Miriam had hit it off. He often stopped to see Miriam at Spence's when he grabbed lunch between appointments.

"Remember, your aunt Martha has her eye on you," Jane

warned. "Don't do anything with that Mennonite boy that I wouldn't."

"It's lemonade," Ruth defended. "They just talk horses."

"*Ya.* Horses." Mary rolled her eyes. "You know what they say about those Mennonites. She just better keep her *Kapp* on."

Dorcas laughed, too, although Ruth wasn't certain she got the joke. Dorcas wasn't exactly slow, but neither was she as quick-witted or as daring as Charley's sister or Jane. Ruth often thought that Dorcas acted and, worse, appeared closer to forty than twenty.

It didn't help that Aunt Martha, who made all of Dorcas's clothing, was frugal and not the most skillful seamstress. Dorcas's dresses usually were made over from secondhand ones Aunt Martha acquired when someone passed away. It was a shame, really. Although no one could accuse Dorcas of being anything but Plain, she did have nice eyes.

Mam thought that clothing that fit her niece better would improve her appearance and attitude by leaps and bounds. It might even help Dorcas to find a husband. The truth was, there were always more available young Amish women than marriageable Amish men, and Dorcas's chances were hardly better than Anna's.

Together, the four girls walked past a table laden with dusty glass knickknacks and tattered paperback books. There were stands selling DVDs and records and even used children's clothing, as well as fruit and vegetables. Tables of toys stood side by side with those lined with belts and wallets. One booth was hung with robelike dresses from the far side of the world. An Amish boy from another church district stood amid the garments, fingering one and talking to the proprietor. He seemed to be attempting to get the man to lower the price, but what the boy would do with the foreign-looking dress, Ruth had no idea.

She liked coming to Spence's, and she enjoyed spending time with Mary, Dorcas and Jane. She was the eldest of the four, but they always had fun together. Even Dorcas rarely whined or fussed when Jane and Mary were a part of the group. The cousins were too upbeat and full of fun to put up with Dorcas's sullen moods.

"So," Jane said, clasping Ruth's hand and smiling up at her. "Tell me. What is Eli like? Have you ridden on his motorbike?"

Mary laughed. "Has he tried to steal a kiss?"

"I don't want to talk about him." Ruth's tone sounded sharper than she'd intended. She didn't want to offend her friends, but Eli wasn't a subject she was willing to discuss right now. Maybe not ever.

Jane must have realized that Eli was a sensitive subject because she quickly turned the jest on her cousin. "Maybe you should ask Mary why she's so interested in kissing." She linked her arm through Mary's. "Charley said she was awfully friendly with that Kentucky boy who's visiting at Silas Troyer's. Charley said she served him three slices of strawberry pie and four cups of coffee at dinner after services on Sunday."

"He needed the coffee after all that ham *you* served him," Mary said. "And he likes pie."

"I'll admit he wasn't hard to look at," Jane said.

"And he was really nice," Mary defended. "Silas said..."

As the girls walked, Ruth's thoughts drifted. She spotted an English woman in her thirties, with the same round face and distinctive eyes as Susanna's. She was carrying a shopping bag of vegetables for an older woman who had to be her mother, and the two were laughing as they walked between the stalls.

Ruth thought about an incident at dinner the night before. Susanna had been carrying a bowl of steaming potato soup to the table and had tumbled and spilled the soup over herself, burning one wrist and her ankle. By the grace of God, her dress, apron and stockings had protected her skin from serious burns, but her wrist had taken the worst of the spill.

Whenever Susanna hurt herself, she dissolved into tears. Luckily, Ruth had been in the room and been able to put her sister's wrist under running water to wash away the hot soup. A little ice and some soothing cream on her ankle had dried Susanna's tears, and they'd been able to eat supper before everything was cold. But the incident had reminded Ruth just how challenged her little sister was. What if she'd burned herself cooking while Mam was at school? What if she accidentally started a fire? Mam couldn't be in two places at once, and once Miriam and Anna married, if Anna could ever find a husband, the burden of caring for Susanna would fall on her mother. Like the woman with Down syndrome Ruth had just seen, Susanna would need supervised care the rest of her life.

Mam must have been thinking the same thing because after the incident the previous night, she'd stopped outside Ruth's bedroom door on the way to bed and hugged her tightly. "You're my rock," Mam had murmured. "I don't know what I would do without you."

"Ruth? Hello, Ruth?" Chuckling, Jane waved a hand in front of her face.

"I'm having black forest ham and cheddar on a sesame roll," Dorcas said. "What about you, Ruth?"

Ruth looked up and realized they had reached the deli in the Amish food market. The clerk on the other side of the counter was waiting impatiently for her sandwich order. Embarrassed, Ruth didn't even look at the menu on the wall. "I'll have the same."

"With root beer?"

Ruth nodded and followed the others to a picnic table in the aisle. There were coolers of cheese and sausages on both sides. The food stalls were crowded with customers and the high-roofed building was noisy. The odors of sizzling scrapple, baking bread and brining pickles filled the air. There was about an even mix of English and Amish here today, but Ruth was too distracted to pay much attention to the antique hunters and shoppers.

She kept thinking about how frightened Susanna had looked the night before and how much she wanted to take her in her arms and kiss away her tears, just as she had when Susanna was small. The further she removed herself from the feelings she'd experienced sitting on that bench with Eli, the clearer it was to her where her loyalties had to lie, and the choice her mother expected her to make. She had promised Mam that she'd always be there for her, and she couldn't let her feelings for a boy, feelings she didn't even know for sure were real, come between her and her family duty.

"Eli Lapp," Dorcas said. She smiled, showing a broken front tooth.

Startled to hear his name while she was thinking about him, Ruth looked across the picnic table at her cousin. "What about him?"

Jane giggled and pointed. "Behind you. It's Eli Lapp. Hello, Eli Lapp."

"Want to have lunch with us, Eli Lapp?" Mary offered, joining in on the joke. She scooted over on the bench to make room for him.

Ruth felt Eli's hand on her shoulder, and for a moment she froze.

"Sorry, I can't," he said kindly to Mary. He looked down at Ruth, his hand still on her shoulder. "I need to talk to you. I went by the house, but Susanna said you—"

"You shouldn't have come here," Ruth stammered, getting up and taking a step back so he couldn't touch her. She just couldn't stand feeling the warmth of his skin against hers. She just couldn't. "This isn't…" She looked around, thinking they should move somewhere more private, but that would only make this harder on both of them.

Mary popped up from the bench. "Oh, I think our sandwiches are ready. I'll get them."

Ruth looked at Eli and then averted her gaze. The lunch area was loud, and the voices buzzed around her. "This isn't the place to talk."

He tried to catch her hand, but she didn't let him. "Then where is? I have to talk to you. I need to—"

"I can't do this," she whispered, interrupting him. There was a lump in her throat that warned her that she was close to tears. It seemed like everyone was staring at them, English and Amish. "Eli, I'm sorry if I let you think—"

"Ruth." He didn't let her finish, and when she looked into his eyes, he seemed to be pleading with her.

These feelings aren't real, she told herself. *It's infatuation. Nothing more.* "Please don't make this hard," she asked him. "Just go."

"A couple of minutes. That's all I need."

She sat down on the bench and swung her legs under the table. Dorcas was staring at them, hanging on every word. Aunt Martha would know what had transpired between Ruth and Eli by supper. *Good,* Ruth thought. *Then everyone will know and the matter will be settled; there was nothing between her and the boy from Belleville.* "You should go, Eli."

"You won't even let me—"

"*Ne,* Eli." She presented her back to him so she wouldn't see the hurt look in his blue eyes, the pain she could hear in his voice. "You're a nice boy, but we were friends, nothing more. And I think it's better if we don't see each other at all…for a while. So…so people don't think we…"

"So people don't think what? That we like each other? Because we do, Ruth."

"*We* don't." Ruth knotted her fingers together, her hands resting on the table. "Just go."

He stood there for another moment and then turned and stalked way, nearly colliding with Mary, her arms full of sandwiches and sodas.

"Aren't you staying?" she called after him, turning with the tray in her arms.

Eli didn't look back.

Two days later, after supper, Eli returned to the Yoder farm. His pride was still smarting from what had happened at Spence's right in front of half the people he knew in Seven Poplars, but he wasn't ready to give up yet. Hopefully, Ruth had just been upset about being caught holding hands at the chair shop, and once they talked, everything would be okay between them. Hopefully, they would be better than okay.

Hannah was right. It had been inappropriate for he and Ruth to be holding hands, and he had endangered Ruth's reputation by his actions. He needed to do this right. As soon as Ruth gave her permission, he intended to ask Hannah for permission to court her.

Ruth was in the garden with Anna and Miriam. As he walked up the lane, he saw the three sisters and Irwin

Beachy. He knew Ruth saw him, but when he reached the garden gate, she was gone.

"She's in the house," Anna said. He knew by her expression that Ruth had told her she didn't want to talk to him, but he walked to the back porch and knocked just the same.

Hannah answered the door.

"I've come to see Ruth," he said.

Her mother shook her head. "I'm sorry, Eli. She doesn't want to talk to you."

"Is it you or her who doesn't want me here?" He shuffled his feet, feeling like a boy in front of his teacher. "It's important."

Upstairs on the second floor, a window slammed shut. Eli looked up, knowing Ruth had been there looking down at him. He could feel his throat and cheeks flush with heat. Ruth must still be angry with him for getting her in trouble. Why wouldn't she give him a chance to apologize? His gut twisted. Maybe it had been a mistake to come today, but he couldn't help it. He had to see her. He had to make the attempt to set things right between them, and he wouldn't believe that she didn't want to see him…that she didn't feel the same way he did.

"She doesn't want to talk to you. Not today."

Irwin came around the corner of the house with the puppy that Ruth and he had found in the hedgerow. The little dog still looked thin, but its eyes were shining, and a pink tongue flicked Irwin's arm. "He's better," Irwin said, holding it up for Eli to see. "He eats good."

Eli stopped to pet the pup as he came down the steps. Irwin was holding it as carefully as if it were a real baby. "You're gentle with him," Eli said.

"I know about dogs." The boy looked up earnestly. "I had one of my own once."

"And you'll have another if you're not careful," Hannah said, following them out onto the stoop. "I never saw an animal take to a boy more."

Irwin came as close to a smile as Eli had ever seen.

"Irwin's going to train him for us," Hannah explained. "It will be good to have a watchdog around here again."

Eli scuffed his boots in the hard-packed dirt. "Tell Ruth I asked for her, will you?"

"She don't want you here," Irwin announced matter-of-factly. "She said so."

Hannah smiled. "You come again another time, Eli. And we'll talk, just you and me."

"No need if Ruth doesn't want me here," he answered, feeling a dull hollowness in his belly. He couldn't remember crossing their yard, but he was certain that he felt Ruth watching him from the window as he walked down the lane.

Ruth woke just after sunrise on Saturday morning to hear raindrops pattering on her bedroom windows. She raised the shades to find the garden and fields hazy and wet, a perfect day, considering the restless sleep she'd gotten last night. She'd made her decision, and she wasn't about to change her mind. But that didn't keep thoughts of Eli from troubling her dreams and conscience. It broke her heart to hurt him, but if someone had to suffer, better him than Mam and Susanna.

She dressed quickly and made her bed. It was nice being the oldest and having a room to herself since Johanna had married and moved away. She'd always loved this room. With the corner windows, white curtains and the braided rag rug, it was bright and cozy, even on a dreary day. She folded her nightdress and tucked it into a dresser drawer, then did up her hair and covered it with a starched *Kapp*.

With all this rain, Ruth was glad she and Miriam had picked berries before dark. Otherwise, they would have had to do it in the wet, because Mam had asked them to put up strawberry jam this morning. They used a lot of jam through the year and always liked to have extra to share with young couples and those in need in the community. Ruth had decided to put some in fancy jars and add gingham ruffles to the lids for sale to the English. She'd seen small containers of grape jelly going for ridiculous amounts of money at some of the stores in town. Strawberry jam would bring just as much, perhaps more.

They were just finishing breakfast when Ruth heard the sound of wagon wheels on the gravel drive. She went to the window and looked out. It had stopped raining, but the sky was still cloudy and gray. "Looks like Roman," she called back to the kitchen. Eli sat on the wagon seat beside him, but she didn't mention that. As foolish as she knew she was being, she didn't want to say his name because if she did, she'd start to struggle with her feelings for him. Just speaking his name aloud made her as giddy as a fifteen-year-old, and whatever ailed her, there was no sense in making it worse.

"He's coming to repair the milk house floor and start on the bookshelves," Mam explained. "He said he'd be here the next rainy day. Guess that's today."

When Dat had been alive, they'd kept enough milking cows to sell milk to a dairy. Now Mam had gotten it into her head to fix the little building up as a library, so that her neighbors could come and borrow books whenever they liked. Both of her parents had loved to read, and they owned more books than anyone she knew. Susanna was thrilled with the idea because Mam had promised her that she could hold the post of librarian. It would be her job to keep the books safe and return them to the proper section.

"My lib-ary!" Susanna exclaimed, clapping her hands. "Today!"

"That's right, today," Mam agreed, rising from her chair at the table. "A lot to do today, Susanna. Working men have to be fed."

"Have to be fed," Susanna echoed happily.

Eli will probably be building the shelves, Ruth thought, gathering dirty dishes from the table. *Great.* She didn't want to see him today, any more than she had on Tuesday or Thursday. What she needed was to put him completely out of her mind, and that was impossible if he was working in her own barnyard.

The screen door banged, and Irwin came in carrying Jeremiah. "Took him out," Irwin declared. "Did number one, but not two."

Susanna giggled. "He means Jeremiah didn't poo," she explained.

"Samuel's here, too," Irwin said. "To help."

Anna picked up the bread tray and walked to the back door. "Anyone for hot raisin scones and coffee?" she called to the men.

Within five minutes, Samuel, Roman and Eli were at the table. Anna set out scones, a pan of gingerbread and some of last night's biscuits to go with hot coffee and thick cream. Mam was smiling. Ruth knew she missed Dat and liked to watch hungry men eat. Still, it was awkward having Eli in the kitchen and having to avoid speaking or making eye contact.

Ruth noticed Irwin watching from the corner of the kitchen. He'd eaten breakfast with them only a short while before, but Dat had always said that boys needed to be around men so they'd know how to act when they grew up. She went to Irwin, took Jeremiah, and motioned to the table. "You'd best have coffee and a bite as well," she said.

He looked at her with hopeful eyes. "Just ate."

"Help yourself, Irwin. You'll be helping the men today. You'll need your strength."

Anna waved the boy to a chair and poured him a mug of black coffee. Irwin added in cream and enough sugar to bake a cake. He didn't grab, but somehow he managed to acquire a slab of gingerbread, a biscuit and two scones. He didn't speak, but he followed every word the men said, and when Samuel stroked his beard during a lull in the conversation, Irwin copied his gesture.

As soon as the last crumb of food disappeared, the men got to their feet and filed out. Eli was the last to go, and as he stopped by the back door, he glanced back at Ruth. She busied herself with gathering coffee cups and carrying them to the sink. She didn't meet his gaze, and after a few seconds, Eli's shoulders slumped, and he followed the others.

"That was kind of you," Mam said.

Her eyes widened. Did Mam mean ignoring Eli was the right thing to do?

"Thinking of Irwin. I think he grew two inches when he slid up to the table between Roman and Eli. He needs to know he's a part of our community. When that happens, you'll see big changes in him."

"I hope so," Miriam replied. "Because he's not much help at milking or feeding up. I've got to tell him every step and then watch to see he does it."

"He'll come around," Mam said. "I've got a good feeling about him."

"How many chickens shall I kill for dinner?" Anna

asked. "If they're all sharing nooning with us, we'll need to start now."

"Three, I think," Mam said. "The jam-making can wait until afternoon. We need to put a meal together for the men. Ruth can do the green beans and potatoes, Miriam can whip up a pan of baked macaroni and cheese, and I'll make some coleslaw."

"I'll get the pickled beets and applesauce from the root cellar," Susanna offered, bouncing up and down. She loved company, and she loved helping.

"I think corn bread," Anna said. "That can go in the oven with the macaroni and cheese, but we'll need more meat. Maybe Miriam can take the horse and buggy, drive to the chair shop and bring back five or six pounds of those thick pork chops we froze last week."

Mam had a big chest freezer, but since they had no electricity on the farm, they kept it at the shop. Ruth saw no conflict in that, but she'd once heard Dat in a serious discussion with Johanna's husband about why electricity was forbidden in their homes but not businesses.

"Our faith instructs us to be apart from the world," Dat had explained. "But since we don't live at our businesses, and telephones, copy machines and electric lights are needed to run a business, they're allowed."

Johanna's husband hadn't agreed. He felt that the bishops were wrong to permit the use of electricity anywhere, so he adamantly disapproved of the use of freezers. But then he could sometimes be a difficult man. Johanna had been a happy bride, but sometimes, Ruth wondered if her sister had found satisfaction in her marriage. Certainly, she didn't laugh or sing as much as she used to before she'd become a wife. Maybe that was the way it was when a woman subjected her will to that of a husband. And maybe her own choice to remain single wouldn't be as much of a sacrifice as it seemed now.

Between the five women, they soon had dinner preparations well in hand and found time to start a big kettle of strawberry jam on the back of the stove. Mam and Anna made their jam the old-fashioned way: an equal amount of crushed fruit and sugar. And they always made certain that some of the fruit was green to add natural pectin. The jam took a little longer to cook, but it used less sugar than if you were using commercial pectin, and Ruth thought the taste was better. Timing and stirring were critical, but by the time the first batch was ready, Ruth had rows of jelly jars out of their boiling water bath and ready for the jam.

Whenever Ruth stepped out on the back porch, she could hear the sound of hammering coming from the milk house. As she worked, Ruth tried not to think about Eli, but she couldn't help it. He was right there in her milk house. Any bookshelves he fashioned would be done with care and careful craftsmanship. And whenever she went to the new library to take a book, she'd lift it from a shelf that he'd made. Would they be properly Plain or, somewhere on the farthest back corner, would there be the carving of a saucy wren?

The clock on the mantel had just chimed twelve-thirty when Ruth went to the steps to ring the dinner bell. Laughing and talking, the men walked up from the milk house.

"What's your mam and Anna got good for dinner?" Samuel asked passing. "Is that macaroni and cheese I'm smelling?"

"*Ya,* it is. Have you seen Irwin?" She searched the wet barnyard with her gaze.

"He went to look for the twins. They walked over a little while ago, after they finished their chores at home," Samuel said. "Don't know where they got to." He and

Roman walked up onto the porch as Eli came out of the milk house.

Not seeing Irwin, Ruth called out. "Peter! Rudy! Time to eat!"

Eli looked at her and then glanced away. "Maybe they're in the barn," he said.

"I'll go." She went down the steps and brushed past him. "You go to the table. You don't want to keep the others from their dinner."

Eli didn't listen to her. He followed her to the barn, and when they reached the door, he put his hand on her arm. "Ruth," he began, "we have to talk. I'm sorry for what happened but—"

"Not now, please," she said. "They're waiting for us in the kitchen."

His jaw tightened as he stepped around her and swung the stable door open.

The moment he opened the door, Ruth knew there was something wrong.

"I smell smoke!" Eli said.

"Irwin!" Ruth shouted, running into the barn with Eli. "Boys, where are you?"

A dozen steps into the shadows proved that it wasn't just the gloom of the day that made the barn so dark. Black smoke curled along the wide boards over her head and made her cough. "Fire!" she cried. "The barn's on fire!"

Chapter Fifteen

"Get help!" Eli waved her back. "Get out of here, Ruth!"

"But the children might be in here! And the horses! I have to get the animals out."

Ahead of them in the box stalls, Blackie and Molly were snorting and stamping in fear. Ruth's hands were icy, her heart hammering against her ribs as she ran for the horses. "Irwin! Rudy! Peter! Where are you?" she screamed. Her last words were lost in a fit of choking.

Eli closed his hand over her shoulder, stopping her. "I'll let the horses out."

"I'm not leaving you." A white barn cat streaked past them, its high-pitched screeching adding to the frantic neighing of the horses.

From the gloom ahead came a frustrated child's cry. The stall door banged open, and a horse reared. Iron-clad hooves lashed out, colliding with thick oak planks. Suddenly Blackie loomed out of the smoke, a small boy clinging to his halter.

Eli snatched hold of the child and smacked the horse's rump. Blackie shot forward, lunging toward the open door.

"Where's your brother?" Eli demanded, crouching in front of the shirtless little boy.

"Hayloft," Rudy managed amid a torrent of coughing. "With Irwin."

Eli gave him a push. "Run to the house! Get your father and Roman!"

A frantic whinny came from Molly's box stall. The sound chilled Ruth's blood. The old mare had survived a fire years ago before Dat had bought her. She still bore the scars on her rump and one hind leg. The slightest hint of smoke had always frightened her. Now she squealed in terror.

"The mare!" Rudy cried, running for the barn door. "I couldn't open her stall door."

"We'll get her," Ruth promised as she ran for the stall. "Fetch the men. Keep low. It's easier to breathe near the floor." Smoldering stems of hay were drifting down from the open hatchway at the top of the loft ladder, stinging Ruth's face and arms.

"Help!" came a muffled plea from the loft above. "Dat! Help us!"

Eli sprinted for the ladder. "I'll get them. You let the mare out," he shouted to Ruth.

"Wait!" She seized a water bucket standing by Blackie's stall and dashed the contents over Eli, soaking his hair and clothing. "Be careful," she warned. She didn't want him to go up there, to risk his life in the fire, but she knew that there was no stopping him.

Eli started up the ladder, and Ruth ripped off her apron and held it over her mouth and nose as she felt along the front of Blackie's stall until she reached Molly's. The air was better here, and she spoke soothingly to the mare as she undid the latch. It wasn't stuck, but there was a trick to opening it that Rudy didn't know.

"Come on, come on, girl," she urged. Snorting, tossing her head, Molly bumped against Ruth's shoulder, and she caught hold of the halter. "Shh, shh," she murmured as she wrapped her apron around the mare's eyes. Tugging on the halter, she led the frightened animal out the back door and into the paddock.

There was no way to tie the horse, so Ruth unwound the apron and let Molly loose. Taking a deep breath of fresh air, she ducked back into the barn, closing the door behind her. The big door was open at the far end of the passageway, and leaving this one open would create a draft that would only make the fire worse. "Eli!" she cried, hurrying toward the ladder. "Have you found them?"

She could just make out a figure climbing down. Not Eli, too small for Eli. "Peter?"

Coughing. A child's sobs. "I'm…sorry…I didn't mean it."

Ruth yanked the boy off the ladder. He was shirtless, too, and covered in smudges of soot. "Peter? Are you all right?"

A flood of tears followed. Not waiting to make sense of his blubbering, she dragged him toward the front of the barn and pushed him black-faced and weeping into the yard. Choking, Peter fell to his knees and began to retch.

A quick look told her that the boy was more frightened than hurt. Again she returned to the smoky barn and hollered up the ladder. "Eli! What's happening? Are you all right? Is Irwin up there?" Was it her imagination, or was the smoke clearing a little?

Eli's face appeared at the hatch opening. "We're all right. Irwin is with me, and the fire's out."

Almost at the same time, Rudy, Samuel and Roman came running, carrying buckets of water. Close behind them were her mother and sisters, all carrying containers of water. Ruth stepped aside and let the men scramble up the ladder to the loft, buckets in hand.

"What happened?" Anna demanded, putting down a soup pot of water. "Are the children safe?"

"Is Molly out?" Miriam asked. "Blackie's running loose, but I didn't see Molly. Is she—"

"There's Rudy and Peter. Safe." She pointed at the twins entering the barn. "Molly's fine," Ruth assured them. "Irwin is with Eli in the loft."

"Was there a fire?" Susanna asked, her eyes huge and frightened.

"There was, but it's all out now," Ruth assured her. "Everything is going to be all right."

"Where's Molly?" Miriam demanded, putting down her dishpan of soapy water. "She must be scared half to death."

"Out back." Ruth pointed.

"I'll go talk to her," Susanna said, wanting to help as always. "I'll tell her everything is all right. She likes me."

"And I'll catch Blackie before he gets in the road." Miriam took off.

"What happened?" Mam asked Ruth. "How did the fire start?" Her voice cracked. "Please don't tell me Irwin..."

"I'm not sure how it started," Ruth answered. "But..." She caught Rudy's arm. "I think this young man can tell us."

Peter began to blubber. "We didn't mean to," he wailed. "We was just..." He turned and dashed for the doorway. "And...and Irwin said...and we..."

"Samuel!" Mam called up to the hayloft. "Is everything—"

"Under control, Hannah." Samuel came down the ladder, empty bucket in his hand.

"Then I think we'd best get to the bottom of this," Mam said. "If Irwin—"

"*Ne,*" Ruth said. "Wait, Mam, until we can talk to the three of them together. I don't think Irwin may be the cause of this, after all." Her pulse was still racing. She wanted to see Eli, to make certain he hadn't been burned, but she sensed that this was the moment to find out exactly what had happened.

"How can you say that, after the school fire?" Anna asked.

"Peter and Rudy, come here," Ruth ordered, as the women gathered outside the barn door. The rain had stopped and the sun was trying to peek from beneath the dark clouds.

"And Samuel's outhouse," Anna continued. "You admitted setting fire to that when you did it."

"I didn't," Irwin protested, coming down the ladder behind Samuel and following the women out into the barnyard.

Mam's eyes narrowed. "But you said you did light the fire at Samuel's. Were you lying then or now?"

Irwin stared at the ground. He was a sight. His hair, face, chest and arms and face were smudged black, his bare feet and trousers filthy. He was shirtless, like the twins. Small, indignant red-rimmed eyes peered out beneath a shock of stringy hair. His eyelashes and brows were singed, his hands blistered. "Set fire to the outhouse," he muttered. "Not the school."

Peter and his brother looked nearly as bad, and tears streaked both round faces. Peter was trying to hide behind his twin. Both were sobbing.

"Hush, both of you," Ruth said. "Now, someone tell us exactly what happened here."

"Matches," Peter blubbered. Rudy nodded.

"Told 'im not to," Irwin said. "They don't listen. Spoilt."

"You two were playing with matches in the loft?" Ruth looked from one boy to the next. "Not Irwin?"

Rudy shook his head. Peter stared at his knees.

"Atch," Mam said softly. "So. The truth at last." She glanced up to meet Ruth's gaze.

"And which one of you started the fire under the schoolhouse?" Ruth demanded.

"Him." Peter pointed at his brother.

"Ne," Rudy protested, pointing at Peter. "Peter did it. He wanted to build a campfire like the Indians in our history book."

Ruth used her dirty apron still balled in her fist to wipe some of the black off Irwin's pinched face. She leaned down to speak to him at eye level. "When I saw you come out from under the porch that day, you weren't the one who had set the fire?"

"Ne."

"But you ran away when I called out to you."

Irwin studied the blister on his left big toe.

Eli walked up behind Ruth. She glanced at him, and when he started to say something, she put a finger up to signal him to wait.

"What were you doing under the school, if you didn't start the fire, Irwin?" Mam asked.

"Chased us," Rudy said.

Peter nodded. "Tried to put out the fire."

"He was mad at us," Rudy added.

"Ya," the other twin said. "Real mad."

"But why didn't you tell the truth?" Ruth raised Irwin's bony chin and looked into his pale eyes. The sadness she read there brought tears to her eyes. "Why did you let us think you were guilty when you weren't?"

Irwin grimaced, refusing to meet her gaze. "Who's gonna believe me?"

"There's more to it than that," Mam said. "You were trying to keep the twins from getting in trouble, weren't you?"

For long seconds, Irwin hesitated. Then his face flushed, and he gave a quick nod. "They're just little kids." He scowled at the twins. "Just kids."

"I can see that you were trying to do the right thing," Mam said. "But you should have told me. Because no one knew, Rudy and Peter got away with playing with matches. And because there were no consequences, they didn't stop, did they, Irwin?"

He exhaled slowly.

"Did they?" Ruth persisted.

"*Ne.*"

"Irwin told us to use our shirts to put out the fire," Rudy said. "But it didn't work. So he threw a canvas tarp on it."

"Too much smoke," Peter explained.

"How did you know they were in the loft?" Miriam asked.

Irwin grimaced again. "Didn't. Bell rang for dinner." He shrugged. "Went to find 'em and smelled smoke."

Samuel crouched and opened his arms. The twins ran into his embrace, and he hugged them tightly. Ruth glanced at Irwin. His lower lip was quivering.

"Did you hear?" Anna asked Samuel.

"Enough to know that these two won't make the same mistake again."

Irwin swallowed hard. "You gonna whip them?"

"*Ne,*" the big man answered, "but maybe they'll wish I had." He stood over his children and looked down on them.

"You two go on home and tend to the chores now. We'll talk when I get there."

"What about their dinner?" Mam asked. "I've got all that food ready."

"No need for them to eat with us," Samuel said. "Children don't belong at the table with working men." He turned to Irwin. "But you need to wash up and come to dinner. You've earned your place there."

Irwin's eyes glowed, and he straightened his shoulders.

"He is a big help to us," Mam said. "I've been thinking of asking Reuben and Lydia if he could sleep here—for higher wages, of course. I think we'd all feel better with a man on the place."

"Ya," Samuel agreed. "The Beachys got plenty of hands to help, and I can see how you could come to depend on Irwin."

"If he agrees," Ruth said, looking to Irwin.

Irwin reddened beneath the soot-stained face. "Guess I could do that," he said. "Too much work here for just you girls."

Roman started toward the house. "Don't know about the rest of you, but I'm starving."

"Come," Mam said, heading for the house. "Come and eat before everything gets cold."

Eli touched Ruth's arm. "Do you have a minute?" he asked her. "I still need to talk to you…"

"Mam needs me," she said, folding her arms over her chest. "This isn't the time." She was so confused. She'd promised herself she'd stay away from Eli, but right now, she wanted nothing more than to wrap her arms around him and hold him so tight she could feel his heart beating next to hers.

"You can't keep doing this to me." Eli watched her,

but she wouldn't look up at him. "I don't know what to think."

She let her arms fall to her sides. "Can't we be friends and leave it at that?"

He shook his head. "Not with you, I can't," he said. "Never with you."

She kept her gaze on her muddy bare feet. "I wish things were different."

"Ruth," her mother called from the porch, "are you coming?"

"I have to go," Ruth said.

"Me, too." He nodded in the direction of the lane.

"No." Panic fluttered in her chest. "You have to stay for dinner. If you leave now, Roman and Samuel will wonder why. Everyone will be talking about us again."

"I don't mean now. Tomorrow. I have to go to Pennsylvania, to Belleville tomorrow. That was part of what I've been trying to tell you. Why I needed to talk to you." She could hear the exasperation in his voice.

"But when are you coming back?"

"I don't know. There are things I have to settle there."

"With that girl?" The second the words came out of her mouth, she regretted them. Her knees felt weak. How had she dared to ask such a question of him? It wasn't her place. She had no ties to Eli Lapp. No right to ask something so personal.

"Ruth!" Miriam shouted.

"I have to go." Ruth looked at the house, then at him. All she could think was that he was going away, that she might never see him again. He didn't deny he was leaving to see the girl. What if he was? What if he was going to patch things up between them…whatever there had been between them? "I'm sorry," she said softly. And she was. For too many things.

"You go on." He sounded tired. Resigned. "I'll wash at the well and be in soon."

She turned away, then back toward Eli. "Thank you for what you did. For saving those boys."

"I didn't save them. Irwin did."

Eli might never admit it, but he was a hero. He'd gone up into a loft that he'd thought was on fire. He hadn't thought of his own safety, only that of the children. "It was a brave thing to do. We all know men who have gone into a fire to save someone and not come out." She smiled at him, proud she knew him, sad that she would never know him better. "You're a good man, Eli Lapp."

"No matter what people say?"

She turned and hurried toward the house.

The days after the near-tragedy in the barn passed swiftly. Late spring was always busy on the farm. In a few days, school would be out, and Mam and Irwin would be at home every day. To her surprise, Ruth had discovered that Irwin, who lacked common sense in dealing with the cows and chickens, had a real feel for gardening. He loved pulling weeds, hoeing and planting vegetables. Not only was he as careful with seeds as Mam, the boy had a knack for laying out perfectly straight rows.

That suited Ruth. Her favorite outside chore was tending the flower beds and cutting fresh bouquets for the house. There were always extra flowers to give away and to sell at the auction. She tried to spend as much time in the yard as she could, mowing and making the annual and perennial beds beautiful, but this year, she didn't feel quite the satisfaction she usually did.

Sweet corn wouldn't be planted for another week or two, but Miriam needed help in preparing the field. Samuel had come with his team of Percherons to do the plowing and disking, and when the moon was right, Miriam would hitch Molly to the planter to sow the seed. This spring Irwin would be another pair of hands, and they needed him badly with Leah and Rebecca still at *Grossmama's*.

Keeping busy from dawn until dusk should have assured Ruth a good night's sleep, but it hadn't turned out that way. She couldn't get Eli out of her head, and every night, when she climbed into bed, thoughts of him kept her awake. She went over and over what they'd said to each other the day of the fire and wished she'd said something different, though what, she didn't know. They couldn't be together for too many reasons, but she wished she could have said something to keep him from walking away, looking so sad. Ruth was surprised how much she missed Eli, missed talking to him, seeing him, seeing his handsome smirk. She missed him, and as one week turned into two, she began to wonder if he would ever return to Seven Poplars or if he really was gone for good. Not that she could blame him. Why would he come back?

When Eli had been in Seven Poplars, he'd caused her trouble, but having him away felt even worse. What was wrong with her? Why was she pining over this boy? She'd made her decision, and she had to learn to live with it.

So Ruth tried to keep busy and tried to work hard, thinking hard work would sweep all the feelings tumbling inside her out the door. Or at least under the rug. Today, there would be no time for moping. She, Mam and her sisters were going to Johanna's house to help her clean for an upcoming church service. With three-year-old Jonah and baby Katie, Johanna could use the help. Her husband, Wilmer, had gone with a vanload of mourners to Indiana to the funeral of a great-uncle and would be away for four days. No one said anything out loud, but Ruth and all her sisters, including Johanna, seemed to be relieved he was gone for a few days.

For an Amish man, Wilmer didn't like farming much, and he was not much help with the small property he and Johanna rented from an English man. Johanna took care of the sheep, the beehives and the hundred baby turkeys. She milked two dairy goats and raised game birds for sale to restaurants in the city. And cared for her two children, and put her husband's meals on the table, and washed her family's clothes and did all the work in the house. Wilmer worked in construction, and when he came home after a day's work, he retreated to his workshop or the parlor where he spent evenings reading and writing letters to his relatives.

Wilmer, Johanna said, put in long hours and was a good provider, but he didn't like to hear crying babies or trip over toys. He'd been a serious man when Johanna married him, and in the four years since their wedding, he'd become almost morose.

But Johanna was Johanna, always full of hope and energy. Nothing daunted her, and she looked forward to readying her house for church services with all the excitement of a once-a-year trip to Rehoboth Beach. Johanna loved company, and she loved the company of her mother and sisters most of all. Today would be a wonderful day. They were taking three huge picnic baskets of food, and the housework, shared between them, would go as easy as whipped cream on one of Anna's pumpkin pies.

The morning flew by in a flurry of soapsuds, buckets of ammonia and warm water for scrubbing windows, and the flutter of fresh-washed laundry and rugs hanging on the line. It was a beautiful day, sunny with a cool breeze, and no one minded the heavy work, least of all Ruth. Johanna had a new letter from Leah and Rebecca and kept them in stitches of laughter as she related the newest adventures their sisters had suffered in caring for *Grossmama* and Aunt Ida. The best news of the letter was that Leah was coming home for a visit next month. She'd found another family who had engaged a driver to come to Dover for a wedding, and they'd promised to bring her along.

After a shared midday meal accompanied by warm chatter and laughter, Mam and her sisters all found quiet spots to rest for an hour before tackling the yard work. Ruth took little Katie up to her bedroom to rock her to sleep. She untied the baby's *Kapp* ribbons and was just about to lay her down for her nap when Mam came into the room.

"She's asleep then." Mam smiled down at the baby. She was chubby and healthy, her mop of dark curls the image of her father's. Jonah, in contrast, had hair as red as Dat's, a feature that Wilmer didn't approve of.

"Johanna's blessed," Ruth whispered. She placed Katie on her back and covered her with a red-and-blue quilt Johanna had designed and stitched before the baby was born. For a moment she stood looking down at the old-fashioned cradle their father had brought from his family home in Pennsylvania. A sweet longing made her sigh with regret…her sisters' babes were the only ones her arms would ever hold.

"She is blessed, as we all are," Mam said, still looking down at her grandbaby.

Together they tiptoed out of the room, and Ruth pulled the bedroom door closed behind them. She was about to descend the stairs to the first floor when Mam touched her arm and motioned her to sit on the top step beside her.

"I need to talk to you."

Ruth sat down, suddenly apprehensive.

"I'm worried about you," her mother said. "You seem so sad lately. Does it have to do with Eli going away?"

Ruth shot her a startled look.

"You think I haven't noticed? Or Anna or Miriam? They were talking to Johanna about it after you brought the baby up." She tucked a stray curl under Ruth's *Kapp* as she had so often when Ruth was a child. "Maybe it is time you start spending less time at home and more time with other young people. If Eli isn't the one for you, there are other men who would make fine husbands."

Ruth stared at her mother in disbelief. "I don't understand. You agreed that I should stay single, stay on the farm to help you with Susanna. Now you're saying I should be finding a husband?"

Hannah looked equally surprised. "Ruth Yoder! When did I ever say you should stay at home?"

Ruth's stomach tightened. She felt as if she was falling. A mistake...a terrible mistake. "In...the buggy. After you caught Eli and me together in the grape arbor." She went on more quickly than before, as if, if she said it, it would be true. "You said I had to set a good example for my sisters and the younger girls in our community. That I had to do what was right."

For a moment Hannah stared at Ruth. "My darling daughter, how did this happen? How did I not make it clear to you what I was saying?" Hannah cupped Ruth's face in between her soft hands. "I wasn't telling you I wanted you to stay home with me. That was my way of telling you it was okay to go, to be with Eli if you wanted. My point was, though, that you had to do it the right way. In marriage, in the church. Not playing games or behaving foolishly."

"But you told me about the letter." Ruth caught her mother's hand and squeezed it. "I value your wisdom, Mam. You were right about Irwin and I was wrong. If you think Eli is an unsuitable match..."

"I was trying to help you think independently and not

to listen to what other people said or thought. I told you about the letter so you would have all the facts. I expected you to go to Eli and ask him about the letter."

"Dat wouldn't approve of him, would he?"

Mam sighed. "Probably not, but you aren't like your father. You're like me. When I left my family to marry your father, when I changed my faith for him, it was because he was the one man in the world that my heart told me would bring me true happiness. He brought me my beautiful children and he brought me to God. I want nothing less for you, Ruth."

"Not all marriages can be like that."

"*Ne*. Look at Johanna's. Or Lydia's. They are couples who make marriage work, who take joy in their children and in following God's path. But you need more, my precious one. What if God sent you this Eli Lapp from Belleville? You talk of following God's will. Have you considered that maybe our Lord sent him to you so that you could lead Eli back to His grace?"

Ruth couldn't hold back the tears. Soon she was sobbing, and her mother was holding her as she wept. "It's too late," she managed between bouts of crying. "Too late. I think…I think he wanted to…to ask me if he could court me, but I…I wouldn't even talk to him. He even tried to tell me why he was going to Belleville. But I turned him away, and now he's gone back to that girl…and…I've lost him forever."

Mam pushed back Ruth's cap and kissed the crown of her head. "That might very well be Eli's choice. And if it is, then this isn't the path you are meant to follow. God will never abandon you, my child. He was with me when I lost your father and He is with me every moment of every day."

"But…if I've thrown away my only chance at love…"

Mam rocked her in her arms, her tears falling on Ruth's cheek. "Whatever happens, you will be stronger and wiser for it. But nothing will convince me that your true path is to remain unwed. If not this wild boy, Eli Lapp, then another. I don't know. But what I do know is that you, Ruth, are a woman meant to love and be loved."

Chapter Sixteen

The sixteenth of June dawned hot and hazy, and Ruth awakened with a stirring of hope in her heart. It was her birthday. The sadness she'd felt at losing Eli remained with her, but she pushed it to the far corner of her mind, determined not to spoil the day for her family by pining for what could not be.

Tonight there would be a birthday celebration dinner. They'd invited Samuel and his children and, of course, Irwin, and Johanna and her family would be there. Leah had been able to remain with them longer than she'd expected before she had to return to Ohio, so having her there for dinner would be a special treat. Ruth's one wish was that Rebecca could have been with them, too, but it would still be a fun evening.

The family had never exchanged expensive gifts on birthdays, as the English did, but Ruth was sure that Anna would bake a coconut cake, and Mam would surprise her with some special treat. More important, when they gathered together to share the meal, Ruth would feel the love and joy of being part of something precious.

Deciding to pick flowers for the breakfast table, Ruth walked down to the orchard with the puppy, Jeremiah, following her. She laughed at the little dog's antics as he sniffed at the scent of a rabbit, leaped to chase a toad and barked furiously at an angry wren that objected to them near her nest in an apple tree. Ruth took her time in the warm sunshine, picking fat black-eyed Susans and delicate Queen Anne's lace. Just as she started back to the house, she heard the sound of a horse and buggy coming up the lane.

Scooping up the puppy, Ruth hurried to see who it was. She couldn't imagine who would be there before breakfast. As she came around the corncrib, she suddenly felt as though she'd tumbled off the top rung of the windmill ladder. Climbing out of a neat new black buggy was Eli. He saw her and smiled, and her knees went weak.

"Ruth."

She opened her mouth to say his name, but she was too breathless to speak. She swallowed, trying to say something, anything, but she could only stare at him, clutching the puppy and the flowers to her chest.

How handsome he was in his black leather boots, blue trousers, powder-blue shirt, navy suspenders and straw hat. He looked so...*Plain.*

"You're back." It was a silly thing to say.

"I'm back." He grinned, then the smile faded, and he looked so serious. "I've missed you."

His eyes were bluer than she remembered. "Gone some time, you were," she managed.

"Ya." He seemed suddenly shy, unsure of himself.

"Busy up there in Belleville, I suppose." She was aware of just how silly those words sounded as soon as they tumbled out of her mouth. She must look a sight, barefooted and *Kapp* askew. She put Jeremiah down, and the puppy barked and spun and ran to bark some more at Eli.

"Hey, puppy." He bent and petted the squirming animal. "He's putting on weight. He looks better."

"If Irwin keeps feeding him, he'll be as fat as a pig." She watched the puppy wiggle with pleasure as Eli rubbed his belly. Silence stretched between them.

"It's early, you're about," she said finally.

"Ya." He stood up, slipping his hands into his pockets, looking at her, then the puppy, then her again. "I thought so, but I...I thought you were an early riser."

She felt her cheeks grow warm. Why was he looking at her so intently? Did she have dirt on her nose? She shifted the flowers from one hand to the other. "I am," she admitted.

Again, they were quiet.

"Those for me?" he asked after a moment.

"Ne." She looked up and then laughed, and he laughed.

It felt good.

There were so many things Ruth wanted to say to Eli. Needed to say. Only she didn't know where to start. Finally she just plunged in. "Roman didn't know if you were coming back or if he should look for someone else to help in the chair shop."

Eli nodded. "I guess he should. I wanted to..." He took a deep breath. "I came early, Ruth, because I wanted to see you without anybody else around."

She felt a sinking feeling in her stomach. He must have decided to stay in Belleville for good, and he'd come to tell her. She nibbled at her lower lip. She didn't want to hear him say it. "Your family is well?" she said, stalling. "Your mother?"

"Good. She's good. And my stepfather and little brother are good."

"Good," she echoed, not sure what to say next. If he

was going back to Belleville, was there any point in saying anything? All she would do was embarrass herself, maybe him.

He took a step toward her. "I know you don't want to talk to me, but I didn't want to go away for good without saying goodbye."

Hot tears stung the back of her eyelids. When she'd seen him in her yard, she'd thought for just a second that maybe there was a chance that she hadn't ruined everything, but now...

"I have something for you. Fannie said today was your birthday, so I hope you'll accept it. I made it for you." He walked to the back of the buggy.

She followed him.

He raised the canvas on the back and lifted out the beautiful cherry box with the round top and the carved wrens that he'd shown her so proudly once before. "It's a bride's chest," he explained. "Remember it?"

"Of course I remember it. It's the most beautiful thing I've ever seen." She set the flowers down on the back of the buggy, unable to take her eyes off the piece of furniture. "But...but I'm not getting married."

She wasn't getting married, not ever. But she wanted the chest. The finish gleamed in the sunlight, and she couldn't keep her hands off it. She stooped to stroke the smooth wood. "It's not meant for me. You should save it for your intended."

His gaze met hers across the bride's chest with such force that she felt light-headed.

"You will marry," he said. "When the right man comes along, the man who's good enough to deserve you."

"It's a treasure," she said. "And the little birds..." She tried to find the right words. "It's a gift the Lord has given you, to make something so beautiful."

"Not as beautiful as you are to me this moment."

Her breath caught in her throat, and a single tear spilled down her cheek. She looked down. Stood up. "You shouldn't say things like that."

"Why not? It's true. I've never met anyone like you before, Ruth, and I never will again. I'd never give this to another woman." He caught her hand and squeezed it and let go. "It was meant for you. It always was, even before I knew you." He took a breath. "I love you, Ruth. That's why it has to be yours."

She lifted her gaze. "Then why are you going away?" she demanded, suddenly angry. "Are you marrying that Belleville girl? That Hazel?"

He stared at her in astonishment. "*Ne!* Why would you think that?"

"Because you went back to Belleville. Because…I thought…" Confused, she broke off. Behind her, she heard the kitchen screen door bang. Someone had come out on the porch, but she didn't care. "You *aren't* marrying her?"

"I'm not marrying anyone. It was you I wanted, only you. And if I can't have you, then…then, I have to leave Seven Poplars."

More tears followed the first, and she dashed them away with the back of her hand. She had to say it, she *had* to. Even if nothing would ever come of it. Even if it was too late. Only she didn't know how to tell him she loved him. "But what if I…what if I care for you, too?"

She reached for his hand and clung to it as if she were drowning and he was the only hope she had of living. "Oh, Eli, I've been such a fool. I thought I shouldn't marry anyone." Once she started, the words gushed from her mouth. "I thought it was God's will that I stay with Mam and Susanna and then you came along and I felt differently, but then there was the gossip and then…but then…"

"Wait, go back," he said. "You…you care for me? The way I care for you?"

She looked into his eyes, his face a blur through her tears. "So much it hurts. Only I made such a mess of things."

"Are you saying your mother might give her permission?" Eli asked incredulously. "That she'd let you marry me? If…you wanted to?"

She held his gaze. "She only wants what's best for me. She'd give her blessing if you joined the church. I know she would if you could put the world behind you and your past and be happy being Plain."

"And you would marry me? In spite of all the gossip—"

"I realized I don't care about that. I only care about you. But I'm Amish. I can't live in the English world, and I can't marry a man who didn't share my faith."

He glanced around. "Is there someplace we can sit down?"

"This way." She led him around the house to a bench near the garden gate. Wild roses grew up the trellis behind them, and the newly mown grass was as soft as a carpet under her bare feet. Shyly, she sat on the edge of the seat and tugged him down to sit beside her. "No grape arbor here," she teased. "We're in plain view. We're respectable."

"But I'm holding your hand," he reminded her.

She smiled at him. "Nearly respectable." Excitement bubbled up inside her, and she trembled with joy. Were they really sitting here talking about marriage? Could her world really have tumbled upside down like this so quickly? So beautifully? "Would you consider it? Would you come to church with me? Become a part of it again?"

He raised her hand and kissed her knuckles. "Too late for that. I already joined the church. I went back to Belleville to mend the trouble with my mother, with my family, and while I was there, I talked with our bishop. I met with him many evenings, and he answered a lot of questions that troubled me. He made me look at things differently. *You* made me look at things differently." He grinned. "So last Sunday, I joined the Amish Church."

She touched one navy-blue suspender. "So that's why no red ones?"

"*Ne.*" He laughed. "I sold the red ones with my motor scooter and bought the horse."

She laughed with him. "Not with the money you got from that old motorbike, you didn't. Or did you buy a blind horse?"

"He's a fine horse, strong and smart. Wait until you see how fast he can trot. And this buggy was a gift from my stepfather Joseph. He said that I never had my proper portion from my dat. He's a good man, and he is the right husband for my mother. I've never seen her so content."

"I'm glad. And I'm glad you have such a wonderful bishop, that he could lead you to God."

"He is a good shepherd," Eli said, "but it was your mother that opened my eyes more than anyone."

"Mam?"

"*Ya.* Your mother and Roman and Samuel and you and your sisters." His eyes glowed with emotion. "For many years, I wasn't sure that I belonged in God's grace, or that He wanted me there. But I watched your family and community bring Irwin into your home and love him, despite his faults. It wasn't until I got back to Belleville and had time to think that I realized what I had witnessed here. If there was a place for Irwin in the Plain world, I realized maybe there was one for me."

"There will always be a place for you here, Eli. In our community. In our home."

"So does that mean you'll let me court you?"

"If you'll forgive me for being so stupid and stubborn, for thinking that I knew best what God wanted. You warned me not to be a martyr, to listen to God, and you were right."

"Will you accept my bride's chest?"

"Only if you'll ask me to marry you. Officially." Her heart was so full of joy that she didn't care how forward she was being—that she'd practically proposed to him, instead of the other way round.

"You'd have me, even when you don't know the truth about Hazel and me?"

"I know you, Eli, and I know you'd never do anything dishonorable. You might make a mistake. We all do because we're human. But you'd never desert the mother of your child."

"You're right, I wouldn't." He started to reach into his pocket. "I have a letter from her, a letter that will explain everything."

"I don't need to see your letter," she protested, stilling his hand with hers. "I believe in you."

"But I should have told you the truth as soon as I knew I had feelings for you, and I should have told my mother before I ever left Belleville the first time." He looked away, then back at her. "Will you listen now?"

"If you want to tell me, of course I'll listen."

He took her hand again. "Hazel was my friend, and we went to some parties together, but she was like a sister to me. I was never her boyfriend. Not ever. I knew she liked an English fellow, and I knew she was secretly seeing him."

"You don't have to tell me these things," Ruth said, her heart already going out to Hazel, the girl she had secretly disliked because of the hold she had on Eli. The hold Ruth thought she had on Eli.

"I do need to tell you. It's important that there be no secrets between us."

Ruth nodded and Eli continued. "I took Hazel to a bonfire one night, at Edgar Peachy's farm. There were English there, and she left the party with someone. I tried to stop her but, Ruth, I didn't try hard enough. She was having trouble at home, you know, following the rules…being who her parents wanted her to be. Hazel was always different. She loved school and she wanted to be part of the bigger world. But that night, she'd argued with her father. She wasn't thinking clearly."

Eli sighed, but he didn't look away from her. "I blame myself for what happened. If I had stopped her, if I'd taken her home when I should have, instead of letting her go with that Englisher, maybe it would never have happened."

"Maybe it would have anyway," Ruth suggested softly. "If not that night, another."

"Maybe," he conceded. "But she was so scared when she found out she was going to have a baby. She tried to talk to her boyfriend, but he wouldn't have anything to do with her after that night. So she asked me to marry her so that no one would know what she had done. I liked her a lot, but I didn't love her. I told her I would help her. I would give her child my name, but only if we told the truth first. I couldn't lie about that to her family or mine."

"But, Eli." Ruth brushed her hand over his shoulder. "She told everyone you were the father. And they believed her."

"They did. I got angry, and I let her face her trouble alone. In the end, she gave the baby to her sister, and she left."

"Did you know where she went?"

"Not until I got the letter at Uncle Roman's. Her English boyfriend didn't want to take responsibility for the baby, but his family helped her with money. She's going to go to college to be a nurse. She was writing to me to tell me she is all right and that she was sorry for everything."

"Why didn't you tell your family what really happened?"

"I tried at the time, but they wouldn't listen. You are the only one who didn't judge me."

"Maybe I did, in the beginning." She smiled at him. "Because of those red suspenders and that awful motor scooter. You are a wild boy, Eli Lapp."

"*Was* a wild boy." He leaned close and brushed his lips against hers. "Marry me, Ruth Yoder, and keep me on the path of Godliness. Keep me Plain."

Ruth closed her eyes and savored a second kiss. She was so full of love and joy that she thought she would burst. "Oh, Eli," she began, but then she stopped when she heard Susanna squeal. She opened her eyes to see her little sister scrambling out from behind the rosebushes to run toward the house—her chubby feet bare, her bonnet strings flying.

"Mam! Mam! Roofie's kissing Eli!" Susanna shouted. "Come quick, Mam! Roofie's getting married!"

Chapter Seventeen

For a moment, Ruth sat beside Eli in sweet silence, gazing into his blue eyes, holding his hand tightly. She wanted him to kiss her again, but her heart was pounding so hard that she thought maybe she'd had enough kissing for the moment.

Upstairs, Anna pushed up a bedroom window. "What's going on?" she called. "Why is Susanna—" She broke off when she saw them together, hand in hand. "I'll be right down!"

"I suppose we'd better speak to your mother," Eli said, "before we cause another scandal...to ask her blessing on our marriage."

"*Ya*," Ruth agreed and giggled with sheer joy. "We wouldn't want to give Aunt Martha even more reason to gossip about us." She was so happy at this moment that she thought she might take off like a dandelion puff and float away.

"Do you want to do it now, or should I, you know, make an appointment or something to speak with her?"

She laughed at that thought. "I don't know. That depends on how soon you want to marry," she teased. "If you mean years from now—"

"I'd marry you today if I could!" Eli caught her around the waist and lifted her up. "I can't believe I'm so lucky," he said, "to come down from the Kishacoquillas Valley and find you." He lowered her bare feet to the ground and kissed her mouth with such tenderness and passion that tears sprang to her eyes. "Marry me today."

"I can't marry you today!" She laughed, breathless, playfully pushing on his broad chest. "But maybe you should speak to Mam today before there's more kissing."

"Speak to me about what?" Mam demanded, coming around the corner of the house with Susanna tugging on her hand. But Mam's eyes sparkled with mischief, and Ruth knew she really wasn't angry. "Eli, do you have an explanation for kissing my daughter in front of her mother and little sister?"

"Sisters," cried Miriam and Anna together as they joined them.

Irwin was the last to appear, the little terrier in his arms. "All of us," he echoed.

Eli slipped an arm around Ruth's shoulder and pulled her close beside him. The smell of her and the softness of her skin was so sweet that it made him almost giddy. "We're going to be married," he declared more boldly. "Ruth and me. In the church."

"But you have to be Amish," Irwin said sternly. "You can't marry our Ruth if you aren't Plain."

Mam dried her hands on her apron and folded her arms. "Irwin's right. So what do you have to say to that, Eli? Can you be properly Amish? Can you accept our faith and live by it every day?"

"Eli has already joined the church in Belleville. He's one of us now." Ruth looked up at him with such love in her eyes that he felt ten feet tall.

"Can you be a loving husband to Ruth?" Hannah asked. "In good times and bad?"

Miriam's chin firmed. "He'd better be."

"Or we'll know the reason why," Anna added.

"I will," Eli said. "I give you my word." He held out his hand to Irwin. "I would like your blessing, too, since you're the man of the house."

Irwin's ears turned fire red beneath his straw hat, but he took the offered hand and shook it. "I'll hold you to it," he said.

"I want to be part of this family," Eli announced to them all, still holding Ruth in his arm. "I want to be the kind of man Jonas was and a son to you, Hannah, as well as a true brother to the rest of you."

"And I promise you that God will always come first in our home," Ruth said, clinging to him for all she was worth.

"Then you have our blessing," Hannah said.

"Ya," Susanna jumped up and down, clapping her hands. "And now I will have a big brother for sure!"

"And I will have a husband," Ruth said.

"The happiest husband in the world," Eli answered.

Ruth smiled up at him, her eyes shining. *"Ya,* and the happiest wife."

* * * * *

Dear Reader,

I invite you to join me in rural Delaware in the world of the Old Order Amish, a peaceful people of deep and abiding faith. The Amish that I know are not perfect storybook characters or quaint curiosities in old-fashioned bonnets and straw hats. My Amish are real people with strengths and weaknesses, people who struggle each day, as we all do, to follow God's word and make the right choices.

Sharing Ruth and Eli's courtship with you is a joy. Theirs is a special love story played against the backdrop of a close-knit, traditional farming community. In *Courting Ruth,* you will meet twenty-three-year-old Ruth Yoder, who believes she knows God's plan for her until the day bad boy Eli Lapp arrives in Seven Poplars. You'll also meet the widowed schoolteacher Hannah, her lively daughters and Irwin Beachy, a troubled orphan boy coaxed out of grief by an abandoned puppy.

I hope that you will come back to visit us in Seven Poplars when Ruth's younger sister Miriam chooses between two very different suitors and threatens to change the family forever. In Hannah's kitchen, the biscuits are hot, the strawberry jam is sweet, and there's always room at the table for one more.

Wishing you peace and joy,

Emma Miller

QUESTIONS FOR DISCUSSION

1. Ruth Yoder believes that it is her duty to remain at home and care for her widowed mother and mentally challenged sister. Why do you think that Ruth believes this is God's plan for her? Falling in love with Eli makes Ruth reexamine her choice. Do you think Ruth was being selfish to want a husband and family of her own?

2. Ruth suspects that Irwin Beachy is responsible for the fire at the school. Why does she consult with her mother rather than taking her concerns to Irwin's guardians or the school board? Do you think that was a good decision? Would you have questioned Irwin directly if you were Ruth?

3. When Eli meets Ruth at the schoolhouse, he is immediately attracted to her, despite his better judgment. He believes that he isn't worthy of her, that a religious girl like Ruth isn't for him. So why does he continue to pursue her against his better judgment?

4. Hannah is a convert to the Old Order Amish faith. Do you think she feels constricted or protected by the rules? Does Hannah seem like a spiritually strong person who knows her place in God's plan? What proves this to the reader?

5. Hannah reminds Ruth not to pass judgment against Irwin without proof. We all make assumptions about people and situations every day. Have you ever formed an opinion and later found yourself wrong and regretted your haste?

6. Ruth's younger sister Susanna has Down syndrome. Among the Amish, Susanna is accepted as God's child and is considered a useful member of her church and community. Is Susanna treated differently by her faith than she would be in mainstream contemporary American society? Has Ruth put limitations on her sister by assuming she will always need care at home?

7. Eli's father abandoned his family and he was raised by a strict, conservative grandfather. Do you believe Eli's mother and grandfather blamed him for his father's mistakes? If they did, did those accusations add to Eli's confusion and rebellion?

8. Eli came to the Seven Poplars community after an incident that separated him from his family and church. If Hazel hadn't gotten pregnant, do you think Eli would have remained in Belleville, or were there other problems in his life? Why do you think Eli believed that he wasn't worthy of God's love?

9. As Ruth and Eli come to know each other better, rumors about Eli's past trouble Ruth and her family. Where Irwin seems to be an unattractive and unlikable person, Eli is handsome with an appealing personality. How do these opposites work against each character in the Amish community?

10. Hannah wants to encourage her daughters' independence, while protecting them. Why does Hannah become so angry when she finds Ruth and Eli holding hands in the grape arbor? If she trusts Ruth to do the right thing, why is she so concerned that the community

not find out? Do you think that single mothers face more difficult struggles in raising children?

11. When does Ruth begin to question her decision not to marry? How did she know that she wasn't bargaining with God because she had fallen in love with Eli? Does Ruth ever struggle with her faith in the way that Eli does? Why or why not?

12. When Eli went back to Belleville, Ruth thought she had lost him to his old life. Why did it take a separation from him for her to realize what she really wanted? Did she take this time to consider her own mistakes in the relationship?

13. If Ruth loved Eli, why does she tell him that she can't marry him unless he's willing to join the church and live an Amish life? Should love for a man or woman come first or should each person decide how they want to live their lives and then find a partner who will add to that ideal?

14. Amish life is constructed around family, faith and community. The desires of an individual are less important in the Amish world than that of the group. What aspects of Amish life do you find most admirable? What do you believe are an Amish woman's greatest challenges?

Love Inspired

TITLES AVAILABLE NEXT MONTH

Available September 28, 2010

HIS HOLIDAY BRIDE
The Granger Family Ranch
Jillian Hart

YUKON COWBOY
Alaskan Bride Rush
Debra Clopton

MISTLETOE PRAYERS
Marta Perry and Betsy St. Amant

THE MARINE'S BABY
Deb Kastner

SEEKING HIS LOVE
Carrie Turansky

FRESH-START FAMILY
Lisa Mondello

LICNM0910